MOORISH CONQUESTS
OF THE DARK AGES
THE WAYFARERS

DAVID MICHAEL DEAN

Outskirts Press, Inc.
Denver, Colorado

This is a work of fiction. The events and characters described herein are imaginary and are not intended to refer to specific places or living persons. The opinions expressed in this manuscript are solely the opinions of the author and do not represent the opinions or thoughts of the publisher. The author has represented and warranted full ownership and/or legal right to publish all the materials in this book.

Mortal Conquests of the Dark Ages
The Wayfarers
All Rights Reserved.
Copyright © 2012 David Michael Dean
v4.0

Cover Photo © 2012 JupiterImages Corporation. All rights reserved - used with permission.

This book may not be reproduced, transmitted, or stored in whole or in part by any means, including graphic, electronic, or mechanical without the express written consent of the publisher except in the case of brief quotations embodied in critical articles and reviews.

Outskirts Press, Inc.
http://www.outskirtspress.com

ISBN: 978-1-4327-7143-0

Outskirts Press and the "OP" logo are trademarks belonging to Outskirts Press, Inc.

PRINTED IN THE UNITED STATES OF AMERICA

This book is dedicated to my best friend Tina Kiebler. Thank you for all the help and support you gave to me during the long editing process.

Contents

Chapter One: Bad Luck 1
Chapter Two: Worst Luck 11
Chapter Three: No Luck at All 18
Chapter Four: The Ludicrous Gallows Thief 29
Chapter Five: On The Run Again 35
Chapter Six: A Major Decision 40
Chapter Seven: The Evil That Men Do 47
Chapter Eight: Identical Problems 53
Chapter Nine: Flight to Freedom 58
Chapter Ten: Sybal 64
Chapter Eleven: Do Unto Others 70
Chapter Twelve: Sybal's Quandary 78
Chapter Thirteen: Teaching the Teachers a Lesson 87
Chapter Fourteen: Faerie Folk 94
Chapter Fifteen: Takes Two to Tangle 101
Chapter Sixteen: Animal Magnetism 108
Chapter Seventeen: Courting Disaster 115
Chapter Eighteen: North Hill 123
Chapter Nineteen: Emotional Entanglements 131
Chapter Twenty: Between a Rock and a Deep Place 138

Glossary

Apothecary - Pharmacist or pharmacy.

Beadle - A Beadle is a minor parish official whose duties include ushering, and preserving order at church services. This sometimes can include performing civil functions for small towns.

Cudgel - A short stout heavy stick or club used as a weapon.

Druid - A priest in ancient Celtic religion: a priest in an ancient religion practiced in Britain, Ireland, and Gaul until the people of those areas were converted to Christianity.

Dowcemere – A dowcemere is an instrument played with lightweight hammers or sometimes by plucking.

Drey - A drey is a squirrel's nest of twigs in a tree.

Fava Bean - The Fava Bean has been cultivated for centuries and is still considered a staple of the Mediterranean diet. Also known in English as the Broad Bean or Horse Bean, it was the only bean known to Europe before contact with the new world. The fava resembles such shell beans as limas and butterbeans, but it is actually more closely related to the pea family.

Garb – Garb means to put clothes on. This includes apparel, attire, clothing, dress, and garments. A set or style of clothing which can be a costume, a dress, a guise, a habiliment (often used in plural), an outfit, or a turnout.

Halfling - Halfling is another name for J. R. R. Tolkien's Hobbit and is a fictional race sometimes found in fantasy novels and games. In many settings, they are similar to humans except about half the size.

Illuminator – A person who adds colored letters, illustrations, and designs to a manuscript or the borders of a page.

Laird - A minor Baron or a small landlord.

Minstrel - Medieval traveling musician: a medieval singer, musician, or one who recites poetry. A minstrel travels around from place to place giving performances.

Monger - A seller, dealer, promoter, or merchant.

Oracle - source of wisdom: somebody or something considered to be a source of knowledge, wisdom, or prophecy.

Pease - A pea.

Pila - Pila simply means 'ball' in Latin and this was the term used most often by the Romans to describe ball-playing. Some sources suggest that the most likely game referred to was the game called harpasta or harpastum, the "small ball game."

Pinfold – A pinfold is a place of confinement or restraint for animals.

Puttock - Refers to a greedy, ravenous or wanton person. Sometime prostitutes were called this or the word Wagtail. Puttock also refers to some birds of prey like the buzzard.

Reeve – A Reeve is an administrative officer of a town or district, or an overseer or superintendent of workers, tenants, or an estate. This officer sometimes can be a person of high rank representing the crown.

Rod - The rod is a unit of length equal to 5.5 yards, 5.0292 meters, 16.5 feet, or 1/320 of a statute mile.

Sand Boys – In medieval times Sand boys would carry sand from the beach to taverns, inns, and other establishments. These establishments would use the sand on their floors to absorb spills, much like the way sawdust was used in saloons in the days of the Wild West.

Shanghai - To force into naval service: to recruit somebody forcibly into a navy. To trick or force to do something: to force somebody to do something or go somewhere against their will.

Steward – A steward is one who manages another's property, finances, or other affairs.

Trencher - A wooden platter: in the past, a wooden platter used to serve or cut food.

Ziggurat - An ancient Mesopotamian temple tower consisting of a lofty pyramidal structure built in successive stages with outside staircases and a shrine at the top; *also*: a structure or object of similar form.

CHAPTER ONE
Bad Luck

Do I have spirit? Yeah, I have spirit. You have to have that and spunk if you are going to survive in the streets of Haven's Rest. Money and fast feet tend to increase ones chances, but since I have neither, I have to survive by using my wits. My name is Hezekiah, but I do not answer to it, and neither do I go by Plowsman, which was my surname until I found out it was not rightfully mine at all. To simplify matters, just call me Zeke, because that is what they've called me since the day I was born.

Haven's Rest is not very bad, unless you are fortunate enough to live in the Inner City. That's the wealthy side. A side where self-important society nobles strut around like stuffed peacocks, and look down their noses at people like me. Most folks do not agree with my opinion of Haven's Rest, but of course, they have grown up in this city, and they have become almost oblivious to what I find most intriguing. I am just a simple farm boy from a simple family, and if it did not affect the farm or our bellies, then it was not important. That simple way of life tends to make those who live it, fall out of touch with the world in general.

Imagine the moment I first saw this city in the distance. I was in awe and completely dumbstruck. I must have gaped at the massive city walls and towers for nearly an hour before finding the courage to enter the city gates. Now put yourself in my boots when I enter the city. Things I have never seen before in my whole lifetime assail me. Everything that these city folks are just taking for granted, stops me dead in my tracks. I am lucky to have survived walking down the street.

Ignorance is not bliss, though before coming to Haven's Rest, I would have assumed we were at least keeping up with the times. Apparently, I was very wrong. Laughter would have erupted from my belly had anyone tried to describe to me any one of a number of things that is available in this city. My father had tried to, but since he is a minstrel, I had laughed at his stories, and regarded them as fanciful tales. Respect for him kept me from calling him an outright liar, but still, I wonder now what he must have thought of my mirth, and of my stupidity. I may have been born within this kingdom, but Haven's Rest makes me feel like a foreigner visiting a new land.

There has not been time to do much sightseeing, but I have seen many things one does not see on the farm. Just last week for instance, during the Festival of the Trees parade, I was able to see the king ride his magnificent steed through the city streets. It was glorious. Imagine my reaction when I saw an elephant, a camel, or a halfling for the first time. It was quite different from the vexed anguish I felt upon seeing shackled lines of weary slaves heading for the auction blocks.

I have also come to accept magic, and accept people who have a mixture of blood from creatures I have never seen before. It grieves me to know my father had been sincere when he told me his stories held truth, but simple minds are hard to convince. However, one cannot deny what I have seen with my own two eyes, nor will I ever doubt my father's words again. If I could only recall a small portion of what he had tried to tell me, I probably would not have been as dazed and ill prepared when I first arrived here in the city.

Daily life in the city streets, markets, and shops can be very alluring, and because of this, I have spent too much of my precious money sampling an unending variety of food and spirits. I cannot help it, for every time I turn a corner, there is something new to discover. For instance, if I want to know what the future has in store for me, I can visit an exotic woman oracle over on Ash Street, and if I am feeling ill, the surgeon on Yew Street can bleed my sickness away with his leeches. The squeamish usually go visit the monks, or an apothecary to cure their maladies, and some still seek out the druids in the ancient oak grove at Thunor. To me, life in the city is like a year round festival. On any given day in the streets, one is likely to encounter jugglers, glassblowers, artisans, illuminators, tumblers, flame blowers or men walking around on tall wooden poles.

Sometimes they block off the streets for events like foot races, cockfights, parades, and contests. At one such contest, I won two coppers for eating more fava beans than the rest of the participants. Though I truly appreciated the money, I was just happy to get the free meal and have my belly full for a change. I am beginning to believe that if you cannot find it here in Haven's Rest, then you are not looking hard enough, unless you are trying to find work, and that can be difficult for a boy who has as many problems as I do.

Today I wandered the streets trying to find a job, and several times, I had to hide from some thugs who are trying to find me. I am soaked to the skin, dogged tired and I only have three coppers to show for my efforts. This morning, I helped to unload a wagon load of heavy crates for one of the coppers, and around noon, I was able to retrieve two coppers from the mud after a gang of boys plucked an unfortunate woman's purse from her hand.

I had seen the coins fly out of the purse, and had waited patiently until the gang and the woman were long gone. Then, I casually retrieved them when nobody was looking. I feel a little bad about doing this, but the survival instinct becomes strong when you are in my situation. Crime does pay it seems, and though I have not fully stooped to this means of survival, this option is not altogether out of the question.

Miserably, I slink down Holly Street in the pouring rain, and the vendors all look at me expectantly. Some try shouting in an attempt to draw me in, but the more experienced merchants do not even bother. The zealous ones just want to make one last sale before giving up for the day, but my indifference lets them know that their sales pitch is in vain.

The Banished Bard's soggy banner comes into view, but I do not go straight away towards it. The colorful banner depicts a Bard, cringing at the feet of a finger-pointing king who appears to be extremely wroth at the man. There are letters that state the taverns name as well, and I am thankful that I have been taught to read and write. The knowledge comes in handy here in the city, for I have also been able to make a few coppers as a scribe. I stop beneath the blacksmiths overhang, and take a few moments to study the street. I have had one close encounter today, and I am not about to walk into a trap.

Thomas stops to wipe the sweat off his brow, and he gives me a friendly wave. Thomas is a runt of a man, very bald, and extremely thin. You'd outright laugh at him if he told you he was a smithy, but if you're in need of a good door hinge or a cheap cook pot, Thomas is your man. I wave back, but a flash of lightening that strikes too close for comfort drowns out my greeting. The following rumble of thunder rolls off into the distance as my eyes rove the street.

There does not seem to be anyone lingering about the Bard, so with a farewell wave to Thomas, I slowly cut across the street and try not to splatter mud all over my trousers. Caution, another survival instinct, causes me to pause at the front window to look over the crowd, and only when I am satisfied that it is safe to go in, do I head for the door.

The swinging doors swish wildly back and forth when I step inside. This is where I call home. Well, at least until tomorrow. The typical evening crowd packs the place, and the stench of unwashed bodies is overpowering. Being new to life in the big city, I have learned to watch my step, and keep my mouth shut. It only takes one misunderstood comment, look, or misstep to entice someone into jumping on you.

The Bard has a rambunctious crowd this time of day, and stabbings happen to more people by accident, than they do on purpose. Unlike the Inner City, the waterfront is a place where the uncivilized converge. Sailors, puttocks, dockworkers, cutthroats, vagabonds, swindlers, gamblers, and people like me, all tend to congregate in the slums. Most of the people who dwell here are just one shanghai away from becoming a slave, or one-step ahead of becoming a beggar in the streets.

Water pools on the planked floor as I let my eyes adjust to the dimly lit interior. The sanded floor is beyond absorbing any more mud, blood, and vomit, but it is not the owners fault. The endless rain has prevented the sand boys from delivering. When my eyes adjust, I barely get out of the way of a staggering drunk giant who looks very green about the gills. I clutch my purse as he goes by, and then ask myself why. A hustler would really have to be desperate to try to lift my pitiful pouch. Its hell being broke. I am not completely broke, but I am broke enough to have to make a choice. Do I pay for tomorrow's room, or do I get something to eat and plow the froth off a couple ales tonight? My belly growls and I suddenly acquire a powerful thirst. Guess I will be visiting old man Gabriel down by the docks tomorrow night.

An empty table catches my eye. It is by an open window in the front corner of the room, and since I like to keep my back to the wall, I head that way. This is usually a good idea since the thugs trying to find me, would like nothing more than to catch me napping. I am also sure that the villagers who chased me halfway across the kingdom might decide to look for me here in Haven's Rest, so it is a good idea for me to keep my guard up. It is really all my fault though, because if I could have controlled my temper, I would not be in this mess in the first place. It is very disheartening, but that is what you get when you accidentally kill your stepfather, and then let a duke, who just happens to dislike my real father, dupe you.

I make my way to the table by sidestepping those who stumble into my path, and before the next player lets one fly, I dash past the dagger board. Drunken laughter erupts as I pass by a crowded table of weathered mercenaries.

"Will ya looky there! Thought one had to have his pubes to be in here? Hey boy, I think your mammy's callin'," one heckles.

I ignore the insulting remark, and hurry past the table. Sabrina spots me and I nod. She gives me a wink as I pull out a chair in the corner and sit down. It is hard not to stare at her as she hustles to the counter to get me a tankard of ale, so I shift my attention to my coin pouch. I begin to frown after I untie it from my belt, because it is in the same condition as my clothing, well worn and wet.

Sabrina sashays back across the room towards me, and dodges a pair of groping hands. Stopping a moment, she lifts the back of her dress up, and lets the man get a glimpse of what he missed getting his hands on. Misfortune is a curse that plagues me, for from where I'm sitting, I don't get to see a thing. Her bravado causes a deafening mixture of hoots, whistles, and crude comments, and I can feel my ears turning crimson. I am not sure why I find her so fascinating, or why I get tongue tied when she fastens those pretty green eyes on me. She is just very easy to look at, and since I am starting to go through those changes a young man goes through when he sees an attractive woman, it is a good thing I am sitting down.

A ferret-faced minstrel begins to hammer on a poorly tuned dowcemere. I guess the ditty is supposed to be "Roll Around in the Hay", a lively ale drinking melody, but the way this wretch is playing, it sounds more like a funeral march. It is damnable. I do not think the crowd even cares, but since my greatest ambition is to be a minstrel one day like my father, the cad's ruination of the song causes my frown to deepen.

Sabrina arrives, and leans across the whole breadth of the table before setting the frothy tankard of ale down in front of me. The top of her dress yawns open alarmingly, and I get a good look at her bosom. Not trusting my ability to speak, I give her a shy smile, and try not to stare at them while I am dumping out the last of my coppers from the pouch. I press a couple into the palm of her hand, and she teases me by taking her time straightening up. I can feel the heat in my face when she turns away with that crooked little smile that says she knows I was looking. Being that I am very impressionable and susceptible to her charms, my desire for her is escalating into a crushing and loving affection. It is nearly as hard to hide these feelings, as it has been to hide from my enemies here within the city.

Unwittingly, I have made a powerful enemy here in the city, but the start of my difficulties occurred long before laying eyes on Haven's Rest. My troubles began when I killed my drunken stepfather a few months back. I did not mean to kill him, it just happened. To make matters worse, nobody knew that he was not my real father, and he did not know it either. He'd been tricked into marrying my mother.

The deception was a necessity, because being lowborn did not excuse the social disgrace an entire family would suffer if anyone had known her situation. Since she had not yet begun to show, my mother's parents thought it was best that my stepfather remain in the dark about her situation. Therefore, she was quickly married off to him after my real father got the wanderlust fever, and disappeared.

I killed my stepfather because he got drunk and began beating on me for no reason at all. My best friend Turncoat tried to defend me, but my stepfather struck him down savagely with his cudgel. Turncoat was my dog; a very faithful companion, though his name would imply otherwise. As you can imagine, I got very angry. Blind with rage, I began beating my stepfather with my fists. I honestly cannot remember how long I continued to hit him after he fell upon the ground, but when I finally stopped, he was definitely dead, and the bloody cudgel had somehow found its way into my hands. Turncoat was in a very bad way, and though I did not want to leave his side, my mother talked some sense into me. My brother had run to the village to summon help when it all started, and my mother was smart enough to know what would happen when that help arrived. Entreaty your father's help, she had pleaded, so I listened to her advice, and fled.

Within days of my fifteenth birthday, I was on the run, and trying to make my way to a city that was halfway across the kingdom. The journey had been cold and arduous, and it had taken several days for me to get here because I had to backtrack many times to try and throw those who were chasing me off my trail. Those who pursued me had not given up easily. They had come close to capturing me several times along the way, but I am sure either I threw them off my trail, or they had simply given up the chase because it was nearly time for the spring planting. Traveling across the land had not been as fun as I had imagined it would be, and much of the journey had been extremely dangerous. People are not very friendly to folks traveling the roads these days, and at some places, I did not get a chance to speak before they decided to keep me moving along.

A fight breaks out, but Dirk is quick to break it up. Dirk's a huge breed bouncer who has more scars than teeth, and being that he's part hill giant, ogre, dwarf and who all knows what else, he's a brutishly ugly creature. I am willing to bet his family tree has more branches than the Camel River, and that his family gatherings are one nightmarish affair. Despite his unpleasant appearance, Dirk's one you would want watching your back if all hell broke out, and with this in mind, I have made every possible effort to keep on his good side. When they refuse to break it up, and judging by the way Dirk cracks their heads together, I am willing to bet they suffer a very bad hangover come morn.

The onlookers return to their merriment, and Dirk drags both men to the door. Without much effort, he tosses them into the street, wipes his hands off on his apron, and strides back to the bar. Returning to my reflections and having yet to touch my ale, I recall my first few days in the city. When I arrived, I had looked like something the cat had drug in, and though I tried to clean up a bit, I still resembled a back hills dirt farmer. My down-to-earth garb and congenial good manners got me arrested by the gate guards when I tried to enter the Inner City to find my father. All right, I admit I did get a little ugly when they would not give me the time of day, or even look at the documents I was carrying. When I got angry, their attitudes changed drastically and I got plenty of attention. Unfortunately, it was mostly bad.

My luck was still heading south, though I thought for a moment it was improving, because the captain of the guard actually took the time to look at the documents my father had given me. The documents were supposed to help me make a smooth transition from farm boy to respected nobility, but that did not happen. Instead, I spent several days in jail. Lord Byre, who coincidentally is the duke and overlord of the area I am from, was the man who secured my release.

The duke was friendly enough, and at the time, I had actually wondered why folks hated him so much. Granted, most folks think of him as an overzealous young aristocrat, who would probably ascend to the throne by way of deception, but I failed to see how his ambitions would affect me personally, so I gave him the benefit of the doubt. His attitude towards me changed dramatically as soon as we were in private, and at that point, everything went awry. Just when things could not have gotten any worse, my luck really flew the coup.

The duke did not take me to my father. Instead, one of his knights took the liberty to hit me over the head. When I awoke, I was bound to a horse that was heading away from the city, and six knights were my escort. My father had never told me that the duke hated his guts, so my stupidity had afforded the duke an opportunity to get back at my father. To make a long story short, I escaped, and I have been dodging the duke's hirelings ever since. Unfortunately, I was not able to escape with my important papers, and without those papers, I have no way to prove who I am until my father returns.

Foam tickles my nose when I get the courage to take a swig of the obnoxious brew this establishment offers as ale. I do not particularly like their brew, but it is better than drinking the water. Somebody walks past the window, attracting my attention. Lightening lights up the rain drenched street, and I get a good look at the man. Its Wiggot the Sorcerer trying to get back to his shop before it becomes completely dark. Nobody wants to be in the streets past sunset, unless they want to find themselves shackled to a rowing oar, or tossed in an alley with their throat slit. I use the wet sleeve of my tunic to wipe the foam from my mouth and hide my vexation as the bitter brew burns holes in my belly.

I have been hiding in the docks district now for a few weeks. I must admit that it has been a learning experience. People in the city do not treat strangers much differently than the people I encountered along the journey here, and sometimes they treat you worse. Other than just trying to survive, I have been trying to learn of my father's whereabouts so I can send him a message. I have had very little success up until a few days ago, and that is when being in the right place at the right time paid off.

Staying longer than usual in the main room of the Bard, I happened to overhear a man mention my father's name during a political conversation he was having with another man. As soon as the conversation ended, I was quick to make his acquaintance. I spent all my coins to buy him a few drinks to loosen his tongue. My ignorance regarding city politics did not last long, and I knew more than I ever wanted to know before he left. Nevertheless, during the time we talked, I had asked subtle questions regarding Seth, which is my real father's name, and I was able to learn a few things about my father that I had not known at all. The man had asserted that my father was a tad bit more than a lowly court minstrel. In fact, he admitted that my father was one of the king's most trusted advisors, and an important foreign relations diplomat. Once I knew this, it was easy to learn that my father was not even in the city, and that it would be a long time before he would return to Haven's Rest. As fate would have it, he was in the north negotiating peace with the elves of Wynelvenest.

CHAPTER TWO

Worst Luck

Now that I have to wait for my father to return, I have decided to press my rotten luck by staying here in the city. Work is hard to come by, and anything that pays well is tough to find when your work history is as short as mine is. There is not any need for plowboys here in the city. I order another tankard so I can get one more peek at Sabrina's bosom, and while I wait for her to get it, I glance out the window.

Movement draws my attention, and I see a hooded figure lurking in the shadows of an alley next to the Tanner's Shoppe. The hood seems content to stand there in the pouring rain, and this unusual behavior causes my heart to thud in my chest. Have they found me? Just when I am about to make tracks for my gear, hood's twin saunters up, and so does Sabrina. Distracted by the need to observe what these two are doing, I toss two coppers at Sabrina, and mumble my thanks without as much as a look at her. Miffed, she snatches the coins off the table, and stomps off with a toss of her hair.

The hoods converse for only a moment and then begin walking down the street. They stop in front of the Paradise, but they do not go in. The Paradise is not your typical drinking establishment, and I found this out the hard way when I was looking for a room. I also learned not to ask a group of drunks where to find lodging. The price of the room had shocked me, but once I figured out that the room also came with a scantily clad woman, I realized why those drunks had been laughing so hard when I walked away.

The hoods walk down to another tavern, but this time they go inside. Judging by their actions, they are probably just a couple of cutpurses hoping to make an easy score on a disoriented drunk. It is not safe to sit here in the main room for too long, so I drain my tankard, and head towards my room. I dread having to stay in the cramped space that is my room, but if I do not want the duke's hirelings to catch me, I had better quit taking chances like this. Besides, I have been neglecting my harp, and I need the practice. When I get up to leave, a scurvy looking sailor with snake tattoos running down both arms seizes my table. He gives me a cursory nod, and pushes my empty tankard to the middle of the table.

I'm jostling my way through the crowd when somebody grabs my elbow from behind. Whirling around defensively, I stay my hand from drawing the dagger at my side when I realize it is just Sabrina. Seeing me reach, her eyes grow wide in surprise, but she quickly regains her composure and leans in close when I drop my hand away from it.

"What's got you so jumpy? Have I done something to anger you?" I can see she's still upset at me for ignoring her, but I'm also a bit pleased that in my doing so, it has affected her in a way that lets me know she is interested in me.

"No, not at all, I've just got a lot on my mind."

My words bring back her smile, which turns into a pout when I state that I am going to my room. Shouts for service are erupting from all around, and an overanxious merchant begins banging his empty tankard on the table. Sabrina hastily withdraws from me to avoid a reprimand from Jolene, but before she walks away, she gives me a mischievous smile. Now what was that all about?

My belly grumbles out a reminder that it takes more than cheap ale to keep it happy, so I head towards the back counter to order some food. Jolene is behind the counter shouting out orders, and pulling out her hair, which is always how she gets when the tavern becomes this busy. Sabrina had told me that Jolene had been a timid woman until her husband keeled over a month ago, and put the burden of running the place solely upon her shoulders. Seeing me standing in line, she points down the hall. I nod, and she hollers to the cook to fix me a platter. I do not have to say what I want because I always get the cheapest meal she offers, and I always eat the food in my room. I catch Sabrina glancing at me with a playful grin as I go down the hall to my room, which makes me wonder what she has up her sleeve.

Habit has my dagger slipping into my hand before I open the door to my room, but when I open it, the room is empty. I light the candle that I leave by the door when I expect to be in late, and place it on the chest, which also doubles as a chair. Then, I cross the room to check the shutters. The last part of my inspection is the opening of the chest, which contains all my worldly possessions. Everything seems to be the way I left it, so I relax.

The room's not much for size and the amenities are scarce, but it is better than sleeping in an alley. On the floor is a woven straw mat that is nearly free of bugs, and a small chest is beside it. The lock on the chest actually works. In another corner of the room is a small stand with a pitcher of water and a bowl for washing up. An empty chamber pot is beneath the stand on the floor, and though I rinsed it out; it still gives off an unpleasant odor. There is very little room to move around, but cheap rooms are hard to find, so I tolerate the inconvenience. The door does not have a lock, so I bar it by sticking my dagger into a floorboard crack that runs along the bottom of it. I just get my boots off when there is a knock at the door. Sabrina's husky voice follows, letting me know that my food has arrived.

Pulling the dagger from the crack, I open the door. Instead of handing me the tray, Sabrina slides right past me, and enters my room with a disturbing backward glance.

"Please forgive me for just barging in Zeke, but I need your help," she exclaims in a voice that does not match her worried expression.

I glance out the door to make sure that whatever has her upset is not right behind her, but the hall is clear, so I shut the door and reset the dagger. She gives me a good long look at her shapely backside when she bends over to set the heavy tray on the floor, and the longer she fusses over it without straightening up, the harder it becomes for me to concentrate on anything else.

Her close proximity in the small room has me feeling stifled and unsure of myself. I wait for her to tell me more about her problem, but she seems more interested in making herself at home. She takes a seat on the floor, and then helps herself to a piece of bread and cheese. Her casualness has me confused, so I break the silence.

"Sabrina, what kind of help do you need? Are you in trouble?"

She chews a piece of cheese and swallows before answering. "It's probably nothing Zeke, but Westminster's pestering me, and I don't feel safe going home alone when he's around. There's just something about him that frightens me."

It's not every day a pretty girl barges into my room needing help, and since I'm no hero, I'm wondering why all the sudden she's chosen me to be her knight in shining armor. I have seen Westminster many times in the tavern, but we have never spoken to each other. He is the quiet, mousey type that always seems to have plenty of money, and many friends. It is funny how the two go hand in hand.

"Well, you don't have to guard the door. It is not as if he will come in here to defend my maidenly honor. Come on over here and sit down."

I know my face is bright red when I sit down cross-legged on the floor beside her, but she is too busy to notice. I reach for the warm loaf of bread and a wedge of cheese while she divides into the trenchers some pieces of heavily spiced meat. There is no telling what kind of meat it is, or what part of the animal it is from, but it smells terrific.

One does not let problems stand in the way of eating if one does not have to, so I rip off a hunk of bread, stuff the cheese in my mouth, and pull out my eating knife. Sabrina sets a trencher down in front of me and I use the knife to stab a chunk of meat. It quickly goes into my mouth with the rest. Sabrina asks to borrow the knife, and after I hand it over, she applies a generous portion of Jolene's famous honey-butter onto her warm slab of bread.

Chewing slowly, I use the time to think, and cast uncomfortable looks in Sabrina's direction. Swallowing the meat, I reclaim my knife, and share my thoughts with her as I add some of the delicious butter to my bread.

"Sabrina, I can walk you home. I do have a sword, though I never carry it because I get mean looks from the guards when they see me with it."

I can see she is impressed, and she leans in until our shoulders brush. This familiarity makes me acutely aware of how close we are sitting. Goose pimples ripple across my skin, causing me to shiver.

"I don't want you to make that kind of trouble for yourself, Zeke. Westminster is not one you would want for an enemy. I usually ask Dirk to walk me home, but I have heard he has something to do tonight. He likes me, so I will tell him about the problem tomorrow. He does not mind helping us girls when patrons give us a hard time, and I am sure he will intervene on my behalf when I tell him about it tomorrow. I was just hoping you would let me stay here with you tonight."

I nearly choke on the bread I am trying to swallow, and hastily grab my tankard to wash it down. When a pretty maiden invites herself to stay the night with you, choking is permissible. Sabrina misinterprets my strangling noises to mean I am fine with this idea, so she throws her arms around my neck to show her appreciation. For some damn reason, she also slides the platter away from us, though we have barely eaten enough to fill a mouse. I turn my head to tell her I am not finished eating, and that is when I get another surprise. I am not sure if she just meant to give me a quick kiss on the cheek, but when I turn my head, our lips meet instead.

When the kiss ends, and before I can even catch my breath, she is all over me like a hummingbird on honeysuckle. I have never had the pleasure of sharing intimacies with a woman, though I have taken the liberty of trying to kiss a few, so I now find myself in an awkward position. My experience is sorely lacking in this area, and nothing inspirational is coming to my head, so I do what comes easy. I let her have her way with me. Some experiences just sneak up on a person. They do me. Some are good, and most are bad. This experience turns out to be exceptionally good.

I am just over six feet tall, no giant, but I do have a near Herculean build. I would not win any beauty contests, but I am not very bad looking either. A pale line, about a forefinger in length, runs down the left side of my cheek, a scar I got when the biting end of my stepfather's riding whip struck my face. It does not add character. Most girls say they like my eyes, which are a sea green with golden highlights near the edges, and some girls say they like my wavy brown hair, which falls to just below my shoulders. Overall, I fare pretty well in the looks department, though I am still self-conscious about the facial disfigurement.

Sabrina is a waif of a girl that is always full of life, and I am no judge of woman, but when I look at her, my chest gets tight. She stands even with my shoulders in height, and probably weighs a quarter of my weight with curves all in the right places. Her eyes are green like mine, but more emerald, and her hair is a jet-black mane that cascades down her back, nearly to her waist. She has a way of looking at me that makes me quiver like an arrow that has just hit its mark, and the way she swivels her hips when she walks just drives me crazy.

Somewhere between the floor, and the move to the straw mat, our clothing disappears. I find this very appealing, and make a mental note that clothing is over-rated. Suddenly, I panic. It is like the feeling I had the time I met a full-grown bear on a narrow trail. The bear retreated. Sabrina does not. Instead, she gets on top of me, and begins moving her body against mine. It feels good to me, but I am still a little jumpy. She senses my apprehension, and tells me to relax. I try to relax, succeed a bit, and nature takes its course.

Having risen to the occasion, Sabrina begins to fill in the gaps where my education is lacking. I am a fast learner, and Sabrina is a good teacher. Satisfied with my progress so far, she begins riding me like a ship caught in a tempest. I weather the storm, but the squall does not last long. Sometimes being fast at something is not always that good. She's patient, my education resumes, and my performance improves. Somewhere in the wee hours of the morn, we fall asleep exhausted.

I awake the next morning to find her gone. I am a little sore in the saddle, so to speak, but I am eager to begin the day. Sabrina's nails have left me something to remember her by, and I only discover this when I put on my scratchy shirt. That is all I need, more scars. I review the events that have led up to my lost virginity as I piss in the chamber pot, and somehow the loss does not bother me. After dressing, I gather up all my belonging in case I am unable to make enough money to pay for another nights stay, and prepare to leave. Just as I am about to exit the room, I hear someone whispering outside my door.

Warning bells go off in my head when I realize that they are not moving down the hall. I press my ear to the door, and discern that their hushed conversation regards me. They have found me. Rushing over to the window, I remove the bar from the shutters, and throw them wide open with a clatter that starts someone kicking at the door. Tossing my pack out first, and praying that nobody is below, I follow it out in a headlong dive. My body strikes the ground with a force that rattles my teeth, but I roll with the impact, and scramble to my feet. A quick glance left and right tells me that the alley is empty. To my relief, they had not thought to place a guard out here in the alley. I hear the door to my room bang violently against the wall, indicating that my dagger has given in to their relentless assault on it. The noise spurs me into action, and without a backward glance, I start running down the alley at full speed. Shouts follow, but I do not stick around to see if this is a case of mistaken identity. I have a bad feeling that it is not.

CHAPTER THREE

No Luck at All

I take up refuge with Gabriel down by the docks. He has a little shack on a strip of land overlooking the sea, and it affords a commanding view of the ships in the harbor. There are a small number of shacks on this rocky neck of land, and all have sole occupants, like Gabriel, who have done their time on the high seas, but have become too infirm to sail upon its waters anymore.

Gabriel is an ancient and withered man, who claims he's sailed on every vessel in the harbor, been to every known port in the world, and has bedded every kind of woman you can imagine, but poor Gabriel isn't adjusting very well to being dry-docked, and in this he has become embittered. At first, his fierce disposition had frightened me, but I soon learned that he is mostly full of hot air, and that his heart is as fierce as his pride. Gabriel has become a rawboned, wine drinking sot, but since he has been very kindly to me, I tend to overlook his bouts with a wine flask.

The day I first saw Gabriel, I was helping to unload crates from a ship that had come in from Rome. Unexpectedly, Gabriel sauntered up with a sack slung over his shoulder, and began strutting around issuing orders to the crew. Our association came about when the ship's captain began having problems trying to keep Gabriel from boarding his ship. I learned that Gabriel sometimes also had trouble with his memory, and at times, he still believed he was the mate on one of the ships he had worked on in the past. Since I was handy, the compassionate captain paid me two silver coins to escort Gabriel safely home.

When we arrived at Gabriel's home that day, he seemed disoriented to a point that I became worried that he would go right back to the docks as soon as I left him, so I spent the night with him. He did not seem to mind the company, so I took the liberty to clean up the place, and make him a decent meal with what little food he had in the house. Thereafter, I began checking on him daily, sometimes just giving him somebody to talk to, and sometimes making him a good hot meal. Ever since that day, our friendship has blossomed to the point where I knew he would take me in if ever I needed a place to stay. Because of Gabriel, I also earned the harbourmaster's friendship. This helps because he sometimes puts in a good word for me when they need dock workers to unload a ship's cargo.

I again manage to steer clear of the hounds pursuing me, and return to find Gabriel in his bed feeling poorly. He doesn't ask me any questions when I ask him if I can stay with him for a while, though I suspect he knows I'm in some kind of trouble, and for this, I am grateful. He seems very glad to see me, and though I do my best to make him comfortable, he passes away a few days later in his sleep. He had never mentioned having kinfolks, and nobody else at the docks knew of any, so I spent the last of our money giving him a dignified sailor's burial.

I am now completely broke, but things could have been worse. I still have the use of Gabriel's shack, which I can continue to use as long as I can pay the rent. There is enough food in the cupboards to last out the week, and there are several full wine flasks hidden beneath a loose floorboard by the bed. I find no rejoicing in my good fortune in the aftermath of Gabriel's death, and now that he is gone, loneliness plagues me once again.

The day after the funeral, I find not one, but two steady jobs. The harbourmaster hires me to hang from a rope scraping barnacles off the sides of ships in the harbor, and in the evenings, I help clean fish for a monger who has just recently lost his arm in a freak rigging accident. Is it not funny how your luck can do a complete turnaround in the blink of an eye? The money will not make me rich, but at least it will pay the bills, and keep me busy until my father returns.

My struggles to survive may have lessened, but I still cannot shake the ache I feel inside when I think of Sabrina. I dare not return to the Bard, but loneliness wins out, and I decide to take my chances. After work one evening, I do my best to disguise my appearance, and I return to the vicinity of the Banished Bard to have a look around. Strolling past the Bard's windows, I am able to confirm that Sabrina is working tonight. Just seeing her fills me with unbearable longings. I confirm that no one is watching the street, and content myself with watching her work from the safety of an alley across from the front of the Bard.

This went on for several days, and my yearnings for her increased to an unbearable level. Then my luck changed. Returning to the dock from scraping barnacles one afternoon, I spot her across the boardwalk overlooking a monger's display of lobsters and crabs. My heart starts pounding fiercely, and just as I am about to call out to her, I decide to sneak up and surprise her instead.

An ox cart nearly runs me over as I hurry across the street to renew our acquaintance. The driver swerves just in time, calls out a few undesirable declarations about what he thinks of me as a human being, and resumes his course. Fortunately, the disturbance does not attract her attention, so I am able to approach unnoticed. When I come up behind her, she is intently negotiating the price of the crabs she has picked out. Winking at the merchant, I reach around with my hands, and place them over her eyes. I am suffering through a malady with my voice right now that happens to boys my age when they are emerging into manhood. It has the bad habit of breaking up and changing while I am speaking, so with this in mind, I try hard to fool her by making my voice sound deep and manly when I address her.

"Guess who?" I growl.

The merchant seems very pleased that he has a role in the surprise, and gives me a wink back. Sabrina has to think for a moment before answering.

"Zeke!?" she asks tentatively before turning to look.

Oh, to hear her say my name fills me with great pleasure. Sabrina turns around quickly, lunges into my arms, and begins whispering into my ear a number of questions of which I am still too untrusting to answer. Actually, I have forgotten that she would ask me to explain my hasty departure from the Bard, and that she will want to know why those men had kicked in my door looking for me. Love has a funny way of making one forget these minor details.

I am sweating like a fat man in a bathhouse, so I buy some thinking time by suggesting she finish her business with the merchant. Refusing to take her money, the merchant begins sputtering nonsensical something's about love and romance, ties up the crabs with a string, and insists that she takes them free of charge. We walk off hand in hand, and her questions start anew. I am not one to lie, but I do not want to lose her, so I lie anyway.

Clearing my throat, I tell her, "My father owes some money to those men, and they are not too particular about who pays the bill."

She accepts this explanation without question, and then she tells me how bad events are unfolding in her life. She starts by telling me she is moving into a room at the Banished Bard that evening.

"Why?" I ask in disappointment. This news is definitely bad. I wasn't yet willing to tell her where I really live until we get to know each other better, so I have to tell yet another lie. "Sabrina, I am temporarily living on one of the ships in the harbor, at least until it sets sail, and unfortunately I cannot bring anyone aboard for a visit."

"Zeke, I can't afford the increased price of the room where I'm living at now, and Jolene has suggested I move into the Bard. It's really more convenient for me," she adds enthusiastically.

I pretend to like the idea, but make a mental note to start hating Jolene and her bright ideas. I am almost on the verge of telling her the truth, and ask her to move in with me, but something holds me back.

I have been suspicious of everyone since my incident with the duke, and though I would like nothing more than to have Sabrina in my bed each night, I decide to err on caution, and wait until she earns more of my confidence. Thinking on it, while we walk, I come up with a good plan. I cannot enter the Bard by way of the front door, but I know I can climb into Sabrina's window without being seen, so I suggest this to her. Sabrina seems to like the idea too, though I think she is hoping I would have a better plan, and maybe suggest we get a place together. Her disappointment shows, and she looks like she is about to suggest it herself, but my indifference causes her to withhold the question. I pretend not to notice, and ask her if I can come see her tonight.

"Let's make it tomorrow, Zeke. I still have to move all my things over, and I have to work tonight. Let me get settled in first, and get some rest."

Understanding, and feeling a bit guilty about having to deceive her, I wholeheartedly agree with her request. We spend a few more hours in the market, sneaking kisses and holding hands like young lovers are apt to do, but then she has to go. In parting, Sabrina makes me promise that I will come to her tomorrow night. This strikes me as funny, since the hounds of Hell could not have kept me away, but I reassure her by promising. Unfortunately, I do not end up keeping this promise.

After the encounter with Sabrina, I go back to work in very high spirits for Patrick, the fishmonger. He notices the obvious change in my behavior, and by guessing that the change in me might involve a woman, he tricks me into telling him about Sabrina. Of course, this subjects me to a lot of good-natured teasing, but I can tell he is very happy for me. I head for home that evening after work with a fresh pike tucked under my arm for supper and a new bounce in my step. Patrick has given the pike to me with my pay, and has suggested a new way for me to prepare it that I am anxious to try. Memorizing his careful instructions on how to prepare it, and how to make a green sauce that sounds divine, I first have to do a bit of shopping before going home.

MORTAL CONQUESTS OF THE DARK AGES

It takes several stops to acquire the costly ingredients that I do not have at home, but that does not take very long, and soon I am hurrying home to prepare the meal. On the way, I try to whistle out a tune to an ode I had heard coming home this evening, but I am having no success. A group of pila playing street urchins had been reciting the catchy little verse, and it had stuck in my mind. The ode was about porridge, and had gone something like this.

> Pease-porridge hot
> Pease-porridge cold
> Pease-porridge in the pot
> Nine days old
> Some like it hot
> Some like it cold
> Some like it in the pot
> Nine days old.

I give up thinking about the rhyme upon arriving home, and begin preparing the fish and spicy green sauce for my supper. First, I cut off the fish's head and boil it. I will eat it first with the zesty green sauce, a bit of cheese, and a piece of flat bread. Next, I wrap the tail with a piece of linen soaked in salted water, and roast it by bringing the fire to bear evenly beneath the middle of the fish as Patrick had instructed. I will eat this last with leeks, and a boiled turnip. Then I melt butter in a pot until it is very hot, and take the fish straight away from the fire and place it into the pot to fry with the leeks. While it cooks, I prepare the green sauce by grinding together the herbs and spices of pepper, cinnamon, ginger, clove, nutmeg, parsley, sage, and a small clove of garlic. To thicken the sauce I add ground-up crumbs of dry bread, vinegar and water until it is relatively smooth like a paste. I cannot describe how delightful the meal was, but after licking the last of the sauce from my trencher, I belch most appreciatively.

After cleaning up my supper mess, I try to concentrate on my harp, but Sabrina's visage keeps clouding my mind, and I start thinking. It is not something I am prone to do much of, but there are occasions. Too much thinking is not good; it leads to bad decisions, and this is one of those occasions where my thinking leads to a bad decision. Unable to focus, I set the harp aside, and go look out the window. A few minutes pass, and I see a man and a woman come strolling down the beach hand in hand. They stop, and begin kissing in the glow of the fading sun. Their intimacy causes me to head straight for the Banished Bard.

Upon my arrival, I spend the next couple of hours waiting for Sabrina to get off work. I watch to see which door she enters when she finally goes to her room, and I am unable to resist the temptation of sneaking down the alley. I carefully count the window shutters as I go, until I am under the one that should be her room. Before I tap on the shutter, I start having an inner battle with myself.

It takes nearly a half hour before my heart wins the battle over my head, and after taking a deep breath, I hesitantly tap on the shutter. The tap starts a whirlwind of movement inside, and I become fearful that I may have tapped on the wrong shutter. Just when I am about to make a mad dash down the alley, Sabrina's voice, and someone else's brings me up short. A hushed argument follows, and since it seems safe to do so, I wait. I would never have thought that she might have a visitor, especially one who sounds like a man; so many things began to flood my thoughts. My sudden arrival has upset her visitor, but the closing of her door indicates that she has been successful in hasting his departure. I grin, though my thoughts are still causing me turmoil.

Finally, I hear her soft inquiry, and I answer just loud enough for her to hear my voice. When the shutters open, I hastily climb in. By the surprise on her face, I can tell I have caught her at a bad time.

"You scared the hell out of me, Zeke! Do you know how much trouble you might have just got me into tonight? I thought you had better sense than this," she scolds, seeming very agitated with my sudden appearance. She has her blanket loosely wrapped about her, and where it parts in certain places, I can tell she is as naked as the day she was born. Jealously seizes me, and I become upset with her disheveled appearance.

"Who was that man I heard in here with you?"

Without batting an eye, she answers me quick enough to calm my anger. "Zeke that was my Laird, whom I still owe money to from the place I just moved out of. He was arguing with me that I should pay for a full week, despite that I only owe him for two days of this week. I had just gotten undressed to take a nap when he showed up, and the cad insisted on barging into my room. I barely had time to wrap myself in my blanket! Besides, for someone who doesn't want to be found, you sure do take some risks."

Mollified, I take her in my arms. She does not pull away from me, but neither is she being very responsive to my caresses. "I'm sorry, and you're right, I do take too many risks, but I couldn't stop thinking about you, and I just had to come." She relaxes in my arms when I begin stroking her soft tresses.

"I'd light a candle, but the one in here has burned down to nothing. Silly me forgot to bring one to the room when I got off, so we will just have to put up with being in the dark. Besides, you can only stay a little while. Jolene needs some help in the kitchen, and since I need the money, I told her I would help her out. I have to be back to work in less than an hour."

Feeling a bit callous for my intrusion, and knowing she needs her rest, I release her. "Look, I'll come back tomorrow night, and let you get some rest. I should have listened to you. Please forgive me." Just as soon as I finish speaking, an abrupt change comes over her that catches me flat-footed.

Stepping back, she lets the blanket fall from her shoulders, and gives me a hungry seductive look in the meager light. Needing no further invitation, I strip off my clothing, and within moments, Sabrina's all over me like a starving woman on a fresh buttered biscuit.

Unfortunately, my stamina does not last much longer than it did the first time she went wild, and our quick frolic ends all too soon. Sabrina rolls out from beneath me, stands up, and pulls me to my feet. Fumbling around in the dark, I locate my garb, and dress while she brushes out her tangled hair.

"Zeke, I hate to rush you like this, but I promise you can stay all of tomorrow night if you want." Her invitation is music to my ears.

"I'll be looking forward to it," I assure her.

After several heated kisses, and with nothing more to say, she urges me out the window. As I slink down the alley, she blows a kiss at me when I look back over my shoulder. I am as happy as a clam at high water as I make my way towards home. It is a quiet evening, and almost everyone's off the street. My only encounter along the way is with a small dog that growls at me from someone's doorstep. When I arrive back home, I find I have become a bit chafed between the legs, and my crotch is itching most unbearably.

Wondering if I must be growing out of my trousers, and groaning because of the additional expense, it is not until I light a candle that I figure out what is causing my malady. To my dismay, I find that the trousers I am wearing are not even mine! What in the nine hells is going on? It does not take a hammer between the eyes for me to derive a conclusion.

The following evening, and with nothing better to do, I find myself outside the Banished Bard. Gone may be the illusion of love, but I cannot seem to resist the temptation of Sabrina's charm, which draws me to her like a moth to a flame. A street merchants stall acts as cover while I try to catch glimpses of her at work, and battle with the turmoil that rages inside me. At this hour, the street is bustling with shoppers buying their evening meal, so it is easy to blend into the crowd. I buy a hotcake from the merchant to put him at ease, and he does not seem to mind me lingering around while I eat it.

Taking delicate bites of the sweet cake, I notice hood one, and then hood two, walking down the street. I had not thought to ask Sabrina what the men who had kicked in my door had looked like, so I am still unsure if I should be wary of these two. Not wanting to take a chance, I casually try to avoid them as they go by; but they do not go by. Instead, they stop outside the swinging doors of the Banished Bard. Peering around the stall, I see hood one beckon to someone inside.

In astonishment, I watch Sabrina step out and begin to converse with the two hoods. She appears jittery and unsure of herself as they talk, and I begin to wonder if she is in some kind of trouble. One of the hoods unrolls a scroll and shows it to her. I nibble nervously at the edge of my cake, and wait for Sabrina's reaction.

To my dismay, Sabrina shakes her head up and down indicating that she does recognize the face drawn upon the scroll. Since I am close enough to make out the face on that scroll, her response causes me to groan inwardly and panic sets in. It seems the duke has come up with a new tactic to find me, for upon the scroll, somebody has painstakingly drawn an excellent likeness of me.

It is a remarkable likeness, and under any other circumstances, I would have truly liked the portrait. At this moment though, I do not like it, nor do I like Sabrina giving me up like that. Sabrina isn't done adding insult to injury either, and my displeasure increases as I watch her show the hoods where her window is, and then accept a heavy looking coin pouch before they walk off.

Much to the merchants chagrin, I have lost my appetite, and I drop the unfinished cake on the ground. Why would she do this to me? Rattled by her deception, my mind tries to search for an explanation, but nothing seems to make sense anymore. What is the going rate of a puttock these days? I know it is a hell of a lot more than I can afford, but not as much as it is going to cost me to buy a new pair of trousers. Fool.

With a heavy heart, and cursing my damnable luck for deserting me once again, I return home feeling sorry for myself. Since I entertain thoughts of becoming a minstrel, one thing is certain. This evening's tragedies will not become a song or a tale that I will be willing to share with anyone else, ever.

CHAPTER FOUR
The Ludicrous Gallows Thief

I am not one to complain, but my good luck needs to make like a homing pigeon and come back before I go completely mad. Three encounters with the hoods later, and running as if my life depends on it, which it does, I evade a fourth group of pursuers. They do not seem to be having any problem homing in on me. I get the feeling that they know where I am trying to go, because no matter which streets I take, I keep running into them. Thoughts stray through my mind of maiming the artist who drew that picture of me without my consent.

After ducking into several clothier shoppes, I spot a cloak that fits my need. The old adage, if you can't beat them, join them, comes to mind as I nervously wait behind a gossipy elderly woman who is taking her time with the merchant. I nearly choke at the cost of the deep hooded cloak, which now makes me look like I am one of them, but I figure a dead man cannot spend his money anyhow, so I do not even try to dicker with the merchant.

They have run me far from the safety of the docks, and I am now within a stone's throw of the gates leading into the Inner City. This is definitely not where I need to be, and I begin to panic. Sweat is pouring out of me like a melting icicle in the hot sun. Changing direction, I lose myself in the crowded streets, and make for an area called Merchants Row.

The Row is a large outdoor market where one can purchase anything from apples to marbled sculptures of Persian ziggurats. The city charges a modest fee to set up a stand in the Row, but most are willing to pay it in order to sell their livestock or any other marketable goods to us city dwellers. They say if you cannot find what you are looking for in the market, then you are not going to find it. Leading into the market is a busy road that runs along the coastline. This road can take me back to the docks. That is where I need to be.

Stupidity has its limits, but I am still trying to find mine it seems. Today is Saturday, but the more cynically inclined call it Gallows Day. It is a day when Merchants Row transforms into a bloodlust-filled area of people who want to witness the punishment of those less fortunate souls that the city officials have caught, tried, and convicted of serious crimes in Haven's Rest. Again, this is not where I need to be. Before I realize my mistake, it is too late to backtrack, or go around.

Guards, who are there to prevent anyone else from coming in or from leaving, quickly ring in the area. Whilst this is taking place, other guard's lead the shackled criminals through the insulting crowd towards the gallows. Those who do not just hurl curses at the convicted, throw rotted fruits, horse dung, and other undesirable materials at them as they go past. I have never witnessed this public form of punishment, and really have no desire to do so now, but I have no other choice in the matter.

My mouth drops open when my curiosity causes me to look at the five unfortunates as they go by. Shocked, I see someone I know, and it shakes me to the core. Well, I do not know him personally, but I have seen him once before down by the docks. The city guard had arrested him because they had presumed he had been involved in a snatch, and pass robbery of a merchant's goods near the docks. The entire event had played out right in front of my eyes, and what makes it not sit well with me is that I know he is innocent. To his misfortune, I chose not to say anything to help him out because of my own predicament. Fear for one's own safety sometimes takes precedence over the plight of another. It would not have helped if I had said anything anyway, being that he is a Draabitz halfling.

Halfling's are not welcome anywhere they go because things have a tendency to walk off when they are around. Yet, the Draabitz are exceptional sailors, and they are highly sought after by ship captains. Ship captains are willing to pay handsome bribes to city officials to keep the outright banishment of the race from occurring in the city. Therefore, most port cities will tolerate the Draabitz to a certain extent, as long as they stay near the docks. Regardless, many merchants absolutely refuse to do business with them, even those in the Docks District. At any rate, I feel bad about his quandary. I watch as they go by. Of the five prisoners, he is the only one that seems unperturbed about what is going to happen to him. In fact, he seems quite gay. I marvel at this, and find myself liking the fellow.

Upon reaching the gallows, a scuffle breaks out before the prisoners finish climbing the steps to the platform. A brutish looking man commences swinging his manacled fists at the little halfling, and starts yelling things at him. I cannot make out what he is shouting from here, but he does not appear to be very happy. Incited by his actions, they all join in, and a chaotic situation begins. It seems my little fellow's gaiety has pushed the other prisoners over the deep end.

I elbow my way to the front of the crowd, anxious to see how he has fared throughout the ordeal, but the foray is too out of control to tell. All hell has broken loose, and the guards join in the fight. They commence to beating the enraged prisoners silly with their clubs to restore order. The crowd goes wild, and they force me to move forward as they surge closer to the gallows to get a better look at the action. Miraculously, the halfling comes out of it unscathed.

The prisoners manage to make it to the platform without further incident, though the halfling, who is still trying to cheer up his mates, has them ready to renew their assault. His actions have earned the poor fellow the opportunity to hang first, and the guards, trying to prevent the others from ruining the crowds chance to see him hung, quickly usher him forward. Still unfazed, he starts asking the guards all kinds of questions about the gallows. They gag him. I can see the disappointment in his eyes as they drop the noose over his head.

The gallows is a simple contraption made of a single wood beam stretching across two upright beams on a platform, which is about seven feet in the air. A noose hangs from the center of the beam, and over a special trapdoor that opens when the hangman pulls a lever. Beneath the gallows is an area oft times called the pit, where the bodies of the hanged, when cut from the noose, drop down beneath the scaffold into a coffin. The loop end of the noose is a keepsake for the deceased to take to the hereafter. It is the pit boss's job to remove the shackles from the prisoner, seal the coffin, and replace it with an empty one.

The hangman adds to the excitement by making a spectacular entrance that even startles the halfling. I nearly jump out of my skin. In a brilliant flash of light, and a profuse amount of smoke, the hangman suddenly appears. A deafening thunderclap follows the startling appearance, and the crowd roars its approval at the magnificent entrance.

Ignoring the crowd, the hangman then makes a show of testing the trapdoor and inspecting the rope. Finally, the hangman turns towards us, and makes as if to pull back the hood of the cloak. Holding our breaths, everyone grows silent. This was something that the hangmen rarely ever do, for most hangmen wish to remain unrevealed. With a flourish, the hangman removes the hood, and the crowd's dismay mirrors my own. The hangman is a woman!

She is eerily pretty, but unsettling to look at. Her eyes make her thus, for they are almost as white as her skin, and just as cold as her expression. Her hair is golden yellow, and it rings her head like a crown. As she looks out over us, she holds her head high like a queen basking in the attention of her subjects. Satisfied with the crowd's awe, she pulls the hood back over her head, and faces the awestruck halfling.

A priest slowly makes his way up the steps to the platform. He circles the prisoners warily, and stands beside the hangwoman. The hangwoman then issues a command to the guard to remove the gag from the halflings mouth. The guard looks dubious, and starts to say something, but then changes his mind. The halfling was not nearly as daunted about speaking up. The priest did not get a chance to say a word when the gag came free because the halfling was already in mid-sentence saying, "… was really neat. Will you do that again? Hey, an all-powerful sorceress would be able to tell that I *am* innocent. You sure are pretty, but you really ought to smile more. Will you help me? I really did not do it. I swear! Are you married? I might be small for my size, but I have a really big…" The guard snorts, and fights hard to stifle a laugh. His face changes to a mixture of fright, and shock when the gag magically leaves his hand, and abruptly puts an end to the halflings charming, one-sided conversation.

I could not believe his nerve. Here he is seconds from death, and the little imp has tried to flirt with the hangwoman. I think he has lost his mind from the stress, and the result of which has left him babbling like an idiot. The red-faced priest simply makes a quick sign of the cross before nodding to the hangwoman. I close my eyes as her hand takes hold of the lever that will send the crazy little man to his death. Unexpectedly, shouts erupt, chaos ensues, and I open my eyes.

The hangwoman, priest, and several guards are down. Arrows are whizzing through the air like a swarm of angry hornets. The terrified crowd stampedes in the other direction, leaving me standing there alone, and gawking. I am not alone for long. The fight comes my way as hooded figures, strangely dressed like me, clash with the guards. It does not take a gypsy to read your future at this point. Except for my dagger, I am unarmed, swords are clanging all around me, and I am dressed like the enemy who is attacking the city guard. My life expectancy, if read by a gypsy at this moment, would not be very long I fear. I flee as if the hounds of Hell are nipping at my heels, and vow that I will never go anywhere without my sword again.

Unfortunately, the only opening I see lies in the direction of the gallows. I take it. I try to cut under the scaffold, and run head first into the pit boss. Just as he swings a huge club at me, the trap door opens. It hits him squarely in the back of the head, and causes his swing to miss.

Little legs fall through the opening, kicking furtively. The unconscious pit boss falls half inside the coffin meant for dangling legs, and he lies there unmoving.

Nobody is paying any attention to what's going on beneath the gallows, and my conscience will not allow me to forsake the little halfling again. I rob the pit boss of the keys to the manacles, and let dangling legs use my shoulders like a ladder. Reaching up, I unlock his hands first, and give him my dagger. He uses it to cut the noose off while I am freeing his feet. My conscience is now clean, but my slate has yet another offence against society added to it.

CHAPTER FIVE

On The Run Again

Alarm bells are tolling throughout the city to summon more help to the area. Fear sweat pours out of me, and I am on the verge of abandoning this little halfling idiot who is begging me to hold him up a moment more while he robs the dead. Over the tolling of the bells, I hear the tap-tap cadence of drums. Damnation, they have called out the army. To add to the noise, the city guards are using signal whistles to coordinate their defenses. In a panic, I grab both the halflings ankles, and yank him down. "Hey!" he protests loudly as he lands nimbly on his feet like a cat. Spotting the pit boss's club, I grab it, and start looking for an escape route.

Out of the corner of my eye, I see the halfling throw my dagger. It sticks in the throat of a curious city guardsman who has come to investigate the halfling's outcry. In dismay, I watch the halfling hurry over to extract a purse from the gurgling man's belt before picking up the man's fallen sword. As an afterthought, he then yanks the dagger out of the guard's throat, despite the fact that the man is desperately clutching on to it with both hands. I sick up what little remains in my stomach, but I'm given no time to wipe the bile from my lips before the halfling grabs me by the leg of my trousers, and urges me to follow him.

We do not go far before he kneels in front of a grate and urgently bids me to help lift it. The grate protests, but finally it gives in. The halfling eyes me dubiously, and I am privy to the reason why. The hole does not look big enough for me to fit my bulk into, and I am not inclined to want to play in the sewers anyhow. Shouts behind us change my mind. I sit down quickly, drop my legs in, and its anchors away, at least until my hind-end gets stuck. The halfling tries to come to my rescue. He plants both feet on my shoulders, and stands on me with his full weight. This does not work, so he begins jumping up, and down on me. It is my turn to holler out a protest, but the words turn into a cry of pain when my wedged backside turns loose, and I plummet downward like a bolt released from a crossbow. My legs buckle when they hit bottom, and I end up sprawled out on the ground with a halfling riding on top of me. Something stinks to high heaven, and I am hoping it is not because I have crapped in my trousers.

Shouts from above prevent me from taking the time to brain the little imp as we struggle to our feet. Sewer goo covers me from head to foot, and I barely get the stuff wiped off my hands before he starts trying to drag me down the dark passage. I hear arrows striking the muck around us, and since I cannot see a thing, I am not too persnickety about letting him lead me through the dark. We hurry away, and leave the sounds of the fight behind us. I can tell the halfling wants to hurry, but running is out of the question when you are leading around a blind man. I hope that the guard's pay is not enough money to warrant following us down into the cesspool of the city.

Several things are running through my mind as we traverse the dark corridors. Things like, how am I going to get out of here, what just ran across my foot, what is this crazy idiot's name, is it suppose to rain today, and what would my mother, and father think if they knew what I was doing right now? Oh, there were a few more questions, but those just happen to be at the top of the list. When I think it's safe enough to talk, I try to get some answers.

"Hey," I softly whisper as I stumble along beside him," I'm Zeke."

His child-like voice quietly comes back to me from the darkness, "I'm Able, Able Nimblefingers."

My breaking of the silence between us is like opening the tap on a barrel of ale, the flow does not stop, and neither does Able. Unlike a keg, which will eventually run out, Able seems to have an endless supply of constant chatter that never ends.

"Whew, that was close. I thought I was a goner. Hey, thanks for saving me. I owe you one. I owe someone else a big thank you too, but I do not know whom. Wonder why they came to free me; I have not a clue as to who they were. I think that sorceress was beginning to like me. I sure would not mind doing the woo-hoo-whoopty-do with her. I actually think she was going to change her mind about hanging me. Really, she had time to pull that lever before that arrow hit her in the chest."

In bewilderment, I shake my head in the darkness not having the heart to correct his addle brained assumptions. Once I can get a word in edgewise, meaning I cut him off brusquely, I ask him where we are going.

"To the docks, silly," he replies as if I should have known better, "it's our only chance. We can steal a skiff, and ease down the coast until we reach a safe place to put ashore."

I figure this is a good plan, but remember that I need some things from the shack. I tell him what I need, and ask him if he can get us to the shack safely. He says he can, and I feel a whole lot better.

The sewage tunnels can get you from one place to another in the city if you do not mind the rats, and the raw drainage water that can come up to your knees in certain places. It is funny how everyone still prefers to use the crowded streets above despite the convenience in saved time. Able yanks me to a stop, and kicks my shin when I start to say something.

I cannot see a thing, but obviously, he has. What I cannot see, I began to hear faintly. Damnation, and Hell's fire, there are voices coming from somewhere down the passage ahead of us. Guess I should have told Able that there are others looking for me in the city. It slipped my mind. In times of great stress, this is permissible. Had the hoods actually thought to stake out the tunnels too? Able releases me, and before he slinks off to investigate the voices, he uses his hand on my stomach to indicate that I should stay put. This is the very last thing in the world I want to do, but by the time I reach out to grab him, he is gone.

I can still hear the hushed conversation going on in the distance as I try to control my breathing, and stop my knees from knocking. I feel the sudden need to piss. Damn. How does Able manage to make his way through this sludge without making a sound? I find myself admiring the little scamp, and I just hope his luck is not on holiday like mine. The minutes slowly go by, and I refuse to let panic set in. The need to piss is excruciating. What would I do if he ended up being caught, and did not come back? I almost yell out in surprise when his hand takes hold of mine.

"It's me, silly," he whispers quietly as I swing the club blindly at a spot where I think he is standing.

The club does not hit anything, so I try again.

"Hey, stop that!" he pleads softly, but with a bit more urgency in his voice.

I stop swinging, and start softly cursing. I am not mad because he scared the living hell out of me, I am mad because I have pissed my pants. I have yet to hear a tale that mentions a hero doing that sort of thing, and it is upsetting to me.

"Come," he says, spinning me around.

We backtrack a ways before he tells me anything.

"There were two men back there that were dressed like the ones who attacked the city guard. Maybe they are just hiding out until everything blows over. I do not know, but that cloak you wear is sure a popular style. You might want to consider a fashion change in the near future."

I decide it is time to fill Able in on a few things. I tell him the same story I told Sabrina because I am just not too trusting of folks anymore. He buys it, and suggests I lose the cloak before we leave the sewers. He does not seem upset with the tardiness of my revelations, nor does he mention it. I take off the cloak, and hesitate. I am not about to just throw it away, it had cost too much, and I still might need it. I roll it up into a bundle, and tuck it under my arm.

We wait in the sewer until dark. I am glad about this because it allows my trousers to dry out. It is embarrassing enough to have pissed in them in the first place, and the last thing I want is to have anyone find out about it. The good news is that Able finds a shaft with a rusted ladder leading up to a grate above. The shaft is within a stone's throw of my shack, and it is comforting to know I will not have to leave my possessions behind. When it is full dark, we lift off the grate, but Able urges me to wait until he can make sure the coast is clear.

CHAPTER SIX
A Major Decision

The minutes seem like hours while I wait for Able to return. Worst case scenarios run through my head as to the reason why he has not yet returned, and my imagination is getting the better of me. Every little sound seems amplified in the pitch-black tunnel causing me unimaginable anxiety. I grip the club like a lifeline. I am sweating profusely, and trying not to hold my breath while my heart thuds like a war drum.

"Come on out, the coast is clear," Able whispers from above.

"Don't do that!" I hiss back nearly fainting with relief.

"Do what?" Able asks innocently as I climb out.

I swipe at him halfheartedly with the club, not too sure if I want to hug him or brain him. Able deftly dodges the swing, and holds his hands out imploringly.

"Hey, what'd I do?" he begs despondently.

I mumble something incoherent, and leave him standing there baffled as I walk off towards the shack.

"Sorry," he ventures, as he follows me into the shack.

I ignore the apology for a few minutes, and then decide that it won't do me any good to stay mad at him, so I accept his apology. It is not his fault that he moves as quiet as a mouse in a room full of cats.

Using a rag and some cold water from the cook pot, I bathe the stench from my body before changing into clean clothing. Able devours some food as I squirm into the too tight trousers I have acquired. He is in much better spirits now that I have forgiven him.

"What now?" I ask, as I cram a hunk of cheese into my mouth.

We decide that it is safe enough to stay the night and the following day in the shack, because I am positive the hoods have no clue where I live. I have taken every precaution to conceal my identity when arriving or leaving the shack, and I have told nobody at all that I have been staying here. If Sabrina has told the hoods the lies I had told her, I figure we are safe enough here for the moment. Able is not too sure this is a good idea, but finally he gives in to my reasoning.

Late the following morning, Able talks me into letting him go out to see if he can find a boat or a skiff. It is my turn not to be too keen about this idea, but he insists he knows how to get around. I finally relent, and beg him to be careful. He stays gone a few hours, and returns carrying nearly twice his weight in things he has picked up along the way. Able stands no taller than my waist, which is big for a halfling, and he has several other racial traits that do not add up. For one, I have heard that halflings do not have any facial hair, yet Able has a flowing mustache that would rival a dwarf's beard. His eyes, hair, and mustache are coal black, and since his race ages slower than mine, I have not a clue how old he is. I see he has acquired a black cloak of a material that is unknown to me. It is of the same material and color as the trousers and shirt he was wearing when I freed him.

"Its war!" he states excitedly as he throws the stuff on the floor. "The elves have conquered my homeland, and they have attacked Mildenheath."

I am not up on politics, or world events, and I wonder how this affects us, and our situation. I do know, because of my father's involvement, that the elves were very upset at those who founded the settlement of Mildenheath upon their lands. The grass is always greener on the other side, so to speak, so it was just a matter of time before the unhappy people of the kingdom would cross the border and encroach upon the land of the elves. This is the main reason why my father had gone to Wynelvenest. It was up to him to negotiate a diplomatic solution that would soothe the tensions between the elves, and the king. This reminds me of another major problem. If I leave the city, how will I ever get in contact with my father?

Able scrambles into a chair because it is too high for him to sit down on. Before he continues speaking, he reaches inside his cloak and pulls out a pipe.

"The elves have had an abrupt change in government," he says as he taps the pipe in his hand. "Their army general, Zakinis Sy'Wilnf, has proclaimed himself king, and he's overthrown the elves governing counsel. A ship's captain told me that when he was making a quick departure from Wynelvenest, he had seen a row of heads stuck on pikes outside the gates of Ce'Annabreece. Another rumor has it that the head of the king's diplomatic agent turned up in a box, sitting right on King Custennyn's throne room chair! How it got there remains a mystery. I am sure the king has heads rolling over that one."

Able laughs at his own joke, but stops abruptly when he sees the look on my face. "What's wrong? Is it something I said, Zeke?"

Feeling very sick to my stomach, I just sit there in stunned silence. When at last I am able to speak, I tell Able the truth about my father and what has happened to me since I arrived in Haven's Rest. When I finish the tale, Able leans across the table, and places his hand on mine in silent sympathy.

"Have you any other family you can turn to?"

I shake my head no, subconscious of the lie, but unwilling to tell him anything else about my past.

"Listen Zeke, it grieves me to be the bearer of such horrible news, but you're in more danger now than ever. It is anyone's guess as to why the duke would try to capture you, and not have you killed outright. If it is for ransom or blackmail, then his opportunity is gone. With no proof of who you are, you don't stand a chance here in Haven's Rest."

I let his words sink in before asking, "What if it wasn't my father? Could it not have been someone else who was part of the envoy?"

Able puts the pipe in his mouth, and begins chewing on the stem a moment before answering.

"I really doubt it, Zeke. The news I heard was too sensational. King Sy'Wilnf wouldn't make a statement like that unless he had captured, and killed someone who was of great influence to King Custennyn."

I stare at the floor not wanting to believe what I am hearing, but too much of what Able is saying makes perfect sense.

"Able, what do you think I should do?"

Able hesitates a moment to collect his thoughts before answering.

"I was hoping you would ask my opinion, because I have a proposition for you. A large number of my people, led by my brother Grey, have fled the Draabitz Isles. The invasion by the elves had nothing to do with their flight, though it may have provoked it to happen sooner than expected. You see, we were already having difficulties amongst ourselves well before the elves decided to attack us." Able again pauses, trying to put his thoughts in order.

"The story of why we were unhappy," Able resumes tentatively, "is too long to tell, and I will go into more detail later, should you accept my offer. Those of us who were discontent had been making plans to leave the isles for some time, but until now we had nowhere to go. Then, an explorer discovered a valley nearly a year ago beyond the Ember Mountains. This valley, which some are calling Canaan, is very fertile, free for the taking, and is not yet governed by any authority. Canaan is just north of the Ember Mountains, which presumably is land claimed by the dwarves, but my brother has discovered that they have not laid claim to it, nor has anyone else. I tell you this because that is where I must go, and you're welcome to come with me if you wish."

Whilst talking, Able takes a tiny earthen bowl, a ball of course wool, a very dry twig, and some flint from his pocket. Pulling a little bit of the fluff from the wool, he places it into the bowl, and then begins striking the flint sharply against the bowl's edge. When the sparks ignite the fluff, Able quickly places the tip of the twig into the flaring wool. The twig bursts into flame nicely, and Able pauses a moment to light his pipe. When the tobacco in the bowl begins to glow sufficiently, Able takes a few puffs, and resumes telling his story.

"When I left here this morning, I went to the docks. To my surprise, I saw that my ship was still in dry dock. The vessel had left, but a storm damaged it, and the captain returned to the harbor for repairs. I snuck aboard this afternoon to talk to a friend, and to collect my possessions. He had been kind enough to take care of them in my absence, hoping that I would escape, and later return for them. My friend also gave me a letter from my brother Grey. In the letter, Grey stated that they had decided to go to Canaan, and that it was imperative that they begin the journey immediately. Since he knew not where I was, nor how long it would take me to receive the letter, he stated that they would winter at Lakenhall, and resume the journey to Canaan the following spring. He ended the letter asking me to do my best to join him at Lakenhall."

Able holds up a hand to cut off a question I am about to ask.

"Listen first, and hear everything I have to say before you say anything."

Before going on, Able pours us some wine, and takes a drink.

"I have thought this out, and the journey to this land of paradise is far from easy. In fact, it is extremely dangerous now that the elves have made their position clear. Going by sea is totally out of the question. I have been told the elves are attacking every vessel that is not their own. The only way to get there is by going right through the heart of Wynelvenest."

I nearly spew my wine, and give him a look of disapproval.

"Have you gone mad?"

"I know what you're thinking, but what is a little risk compared to what awaits us here. The king's hand stretches far, my friend, and if anyone at all saw you free me, your troubles are just beginning."

I had not thought about it like that, but now that he mentions it, the pit boss had clearly seen my face despite the hood. I suddenly feel unwell as the memory of his face, looming near mine, makes me recall where I had seen the man. He had been one of my jailers during my imprisonment. I find myself not willing to bet my life against the chance that he might not remember me.

"Zeke, if we can get away from here, we can go to Lakenhall. I seriously doubt we will make Grey's deadline, but we can try. If we do not, I am confident we will catch up with them before they reach Canaan. The dwarves are allowing safe passage to those who wish to cross through their territory into Canaan. Crossing the land of the elves undetected is where the danger lies."

Able jumps off the chair, and begins pacing back and forth as he continues speaking.

"Mildenheath is what sparked the elves into closing their borders to foreigners. The elf king feels that the human kings are deliberately allowing their subjects to encroach upon Wynelvenest in an attempt to expand their kingdoms. In retaliation for this, King Sy'Wilnf has declared war upon all the human kingdoms. I believe I can safety get us through their lands because I have done it several times before. If all goes well, it should not take more than a month to reach Lakenhall. We have three months to work with in order to get there before winter, so we should have plenty of time as long as nothing drastically goes wrong. We will wait out the winter storms there, and leave after the last snows have melted sometime in late spring. It will only take a month or so to reach Canaan once we depart from Lakenhall. I have made up my mind, and it sure would be an honor if you would consider coming with me. Just think of the grand adventures we'll share, and the sites we'll see."

Able grabs his cup from the table, and sips his wine, allowing me the time to mull over what he has told me. Was my father truly dead? Even if he is alive, I have my doubts that he can help me with all the trouble I now find myself in. The cards are stacked against me in too many ways, and something inside me is telling me to get as far away from here as possible. Maybe I should do as my father had done, and see if I can make good on my own.

My father had grown up the son of a poor farmer, and he had beaten the odds by achieving his success the hard way. So, could I not do the same? Able is opening a door, and offering me a chance to choose my own destiny. Sure, it would be dangerous, but is not anything worthwhile worth some risk? Had not my father risked everything in pursuit of his dream to become a minstrel, including forsaking a life with my mother?

When I began to show an interest in becoming a minstrel, my father began to teach me as much as he could in the little time that his visits to our home would allow. In doing so, my appetite was wet, and I became hungry for more knowledge. I remember well my father stressing that the best knowledge he had ever received had not come from a book, but it had come from simply traveling about the land. The key to becoming the best minstrel in the realms, he had insisted, was to simply listen to the people, and pass on to others what you have learned. Heeding the wisdom in his advice, I decide to take my chances, and go with Able to Canaan.

CHAPTER SEVEN

The Evil That Men Do

Able, after having sat back down, leaps from the chair again, and smacks me on the back with his hand. It happens so quickly, I nearly drop my glass in surprise.

"Excellent! I suggest we get some rest. We have a long night ahead of us," he says as he unrolls his blanket on the floor, and then lies down upon it.

"How will we get out of the city?" I ask, but soft snores greet my inquiry.

I am not yet feeling tired enough to sleep, so I take up my small lap harp, and strum it softly. The harp is old, its strings are dry rotting, and it is probably not worth a tarnished copper, but it's mine. It is really a child's toy, but it is all that I can afford at this time. I try to practice the exercises my father had taught me, but thoughts of him possibly being dead cause me to falter.

My father and I had spent very little time together, but our affection for one another had grown deep in the short time we were able to be together. I was nearly ten when he first showed up in Blossom, and I couldn't believe it at first when I learned from my mother that I was his son. From then on, he would come once a year, bringing with him enough strong spirits and coin to pacify my unsuspecting stepfather. He would generally stay a week or more, showing me how to play his lap harp, telling me fantastical legends and lore, and teaching me to read and write. When he announced each time that he would have to return to Haven's Rest, I had always begged for him to take me with him, but he always had some excuse as to why I needed to stay with my mother. Stifling a yawn, I stretch and push aside the painful thoughts of him.

I didn't realize just how tired I had become, so trying hard not to make any noise to wake Able, I carefully place the harp in its battered case, and strap it to my pack. Before lying down, I place the wooden bar across the door. When I finally climb into the bed, I sadly wonder how long it will be before I will again enjoy the comfort of a bed, and a roof over my head.

It is full dark when Able taps me on the shoulder to wake me up. While we eat a cold meal in the dim candlelight, Able tells me what this night has in store for us.

"My friend is going to borrow a rowboat from the ship, and row us to a safe point past the city gates. He will meet us at the pier in about an hour. We had better get going."

I sigh, and begin gathering my belonging.

As I strap on my sword, Able asks," are you any better with that sword than you are with the harp?"

Somewhat perturbed at the comment and glad he cannot see my face because my back is to him, I grudging admit that I am not. No witticisms follow the admission, and I am further disgruntled.

"I have practiced with it somewhat, but if you're asking if I've ever used it against anyone, no, I have not?" I say defensively, my voice having a bit of an edge to it.

"Hey, I am just joking. You are not too bad with that harp. I am not too good with a sword either. I'm much better with my daggers."

I admit I have no experience with the blade, for I had found it one day when I was plowing a new section of field. With all the work to do on the farm, there had not been time to play around with it, nor had I wanted to risk my stepfather seeing me with it. If he had known I had found it, and the old coins that were with the body I had plowed up, he would have immediately taken them from me. I did tell my mother of the find, and upon her advice, I hid the things away in a hollow tree.

The sword is a beautiful blade, and despite being buried for who knows how long, it shows no signs of rust. It is rather long, edged on one side, and the guard looks like a poorly made bowl. The pommel looks like an egg, but people who have seen the blade, say it is suppose to look this way. Gabriel had shown me how to wrap the hilt with a strip of cloth to improve the grip, and though he could not teach me much on how to use it, he had been able to show me how to hold the sword properly.

The scabbard and former hilt wrappings had not fared nearly as well, for they had just about rotted entirely away when I had found the sword. My mother had made me a scabbard for it from some scrap leather she had squirreled away, and she had given it to me for my fourteenth birthing day present. Interrupting my thoughts, Able beckons, and I quickly follow him out the door.

We make our way quietly through the streets, never once seeing anyone about. The moon is a crescent in the sky, and it provides just enough light to guide us.

"Hey," Able whispers apprehensively, pulling me into the shadows, and then begins peering intently down the street.

Straining my eyes to see what has upset him, I spot what he sees far ahead near some crates in front of a warehouse. There are three hooded shadows idly watching the street. It is possible they could be warehouse guards changing shifts, but it is more likely they are some of the duke's hirelings on the lookout for me. Taking no chances, Able spots a drainage ditch, and motions for me to follow.

We barely slide down into the deep drainage ditch before a fourth hooded person joins the guards. The waterway is almost as deep as I am tall, and I have to crouch to keep my head below its rim. In this stooping manner, I continue following Able. Debris slows our progress, probably tossed into the ditch by those too lazy to take their garbage to the dump outside the city walls. We travel like this for nearly a half an hour, and Able is becoming increasingly agitated about the time it is taking us to maneuver the obstacles in our path.

A muffled scream brings us to an abrupt stop, and Able glances at me in bewilderment. There is no doubt in my mind that the scream has come from a woman in distress. The sound of a struggle ensues, and men's laughter follows. Able points at the rim, and I carefully peek over it, but I am unable to see what is happening from our location. Then, from an alley between two warehouses, I see a hooded figure. The man looks around anxiously for a moment, and then disappears into the alley. I whisper what I have seen to Able, but he simply shrugs, and begins to walk away. Grabbing him by the back of the collar, which is the only thing I can grasp at quickly, I stop him.

"Hey," he exclaims a little too loud for comfort, and spins around wondering why I have stopped him.

"Look," I whisper tersely, "that sounds like a lady who might be in trouble. We can't just ignore what we are hearing without making sure that she's all right."

Able, dismayed at what I'm suggesting, protests his concern regarding the idea.

"Zeke, there is no time!"

"Well, I don't care. I already have enough demons wreaking hell on my conscience. I will not add another. If it was you, which it once was…," I was so mad, I could not finish.

Able, taken aback at the rebuke, hangs his head in shame. "You're right, of course," he admits, and sheepishly gives me a grin in an attempt to curb my irritation with him, "give me a boost up."

Lifting him over the rim, I swiftly follow. We rapidly cross the street, and ease up to the corner of one of the warehouses. Unprepared for what I see when I peek around the corner, I become very wroth. Four hooded men, halfway down the alley, are molesting two young women.

One of the women is lying on her back with her hands uncomfortably tied beneath her. There is a gag in her mouth to prevent her from screaming, and her robe is open to expose her body. Three of the hoods are taking liberties with her as she struggles in the dirt. They are mocking her in hushed tones, and laughing quietly as she fights to pull away from them.

The last man is behind another exposed and similarly bound woman. She is on her knees, and her robe is laying in the dirt beside them. The man is grunting like a pig as he struggles to remove his trousers. The woman commences to struggle fiercely, but stops when the man strikes the back of her head savagely with his fist. I run the man through with my sword at about the time he finally gets his trousers down to his knees, revealing a grotesquely fat backside. Satisfaction fills me when his grunting noises change to strangled gurgles. He soon dies choking on his own blood.

I whirl around, eager to engage with the other three tormentors, but my thirst for their blood goes unfulfilled. Incredibly, Able has already killed the other three, sending them to hell where they belong. Able wipes the blood off his daggers on the cloak of a dead man at his feet. He nods his approval, and then grins.

Pulling the sword from the fat man, I let my arm fall until the tip of my sword touches the ground. My anger is gone, and I suddenly feel drained of all my strength. Able continues to peer at me, searching my face. I sense, by the way he is looking at me, that he understands the turmoil one goes through when one takes the life of another.

"They deserved it, Zeke. Let it go. You've done yourself proud this day."

I am still in shock as he turns to the frightened woman, and begins to free her. It had all happened so quickly, that I simply cannot recall the moment I drew my sword, and rushed down the alley.

"Zeke! Let it go!" Able's sharp command brings me back to my senses.

When I turn around to free the other woman, I find her curled up protectively and lying on her side. She begins kicking at me as I kneel down beside her, and reach out to undo her bonds. Her eyes are wild looking, like those of a cornered animal.

"Listen, I won't hurt you, and I'm sorry we didn't get here sooner to stop them," I say, stopping to let her hear the heartfelt compassion in my voice. "Please, all I want to do is free you."

She relaxes only for a moment, for when I unwittingly draw my dagger, her nostrils flare, and the wild look returns to her eyes.

"No," I plead, realizing my mistake too late, and barely able to leap back quick enough to avoid a kick to my crotch, "I just want to cut the rope with it. Please, believe me."

The words calm her down, and I cautiously move near her again. When I cut the rope binding her hands, she quickly pulls the gag from her mouth, and spits. I am prepared to dive away should she use the moment to attack me again, but she does not. A look of embarrassment crosses her face after I cut the rope binding her feet, and she dives for her robe. Quickly she puts it on, and ties the belt. She catches me completely off guard when she throws her arms about me, buries her face in my chest, and begins to sob pitifully. Not knowing what to say that will comfort her, I awkwardly hold her, letting her vent her emotions.

Able and the other woman approach us a moment later, their footfalls causing the woman I hold to tremble, but she does not release me. The woman with Able quickly kneels down beside us, and begins to console the weeping woman in my arms.

"Sapphire, let it go," she says echoing Able's words from before.

"Oh, Ruby," the woman in my arms sobs, her voice muffled by my cloak, "how could they do this?"

Clearly agitated, Able stands a few feet behind us, peering up and down the alley. I shoot him an imploring look, wondering what we should do now. Seeing my silent query, he fans his hands out, shrugs his shoulders, and slowly shakes his head side to side indicating he has no idea what we should do. Then, the bells begin to toll.

CHAPTER EIGHT

Identical Problems

The rapid high-pitched dingdong of the bells is an indication that there is a fire somewhere nearby. The clanging seems to be coming from the direction of the harbor. Cursing, Able runs down the alley to get a look at the situation.

Gently, I free myself from Sapphire's embrace, and give her unto the care of Ruby.

"Wait here," I implore.

Ruby nods, and I take off after Able. In the distance, I can see billowing smoke, and a reddish-yellow glow illuminating the night sky.

Returning from his observations, Able meets me midway down the alley, and brings me to a stop near the three bodies.

"It appears that a ship has caught fire in the harbor," he claims as he stoops down to search the bodies at our feet.

I bend down, and pull each of their hoods back, but I don't recognize any of them. I walk back to the girls, and do the same with the hood of the man I have killed, but his face is also unfamiliar to me. Matter of fact, his appearance is of a race I have never seen before.

"Half-orc," Able comments upon seeing my questioning face.

The face is hideous, almost ape-like. The ears are large, and come to a point like an elves, but not as sharply. The mouth is a cavernous affair with two long curved teeth protruding from the lower jaw like that of a dog, or a wolf.

"Look, we've got to get out of here," Able says as he tucks into his cloak the items he has pilfered, "I believe our plans to depart this night must be abandoned. I will go on, and make other arrangements with my friend. We can try again tomorrow night. Do you think you can get these women to wherever they need to go, and get back to the shack safely?"

"I believe I can, Able. Please be careful."

"Good, then I shall meet you back at the shack as soon as I can. You take care as well my friend."

A concerned expression clearly shows upon his face as he turns away and heads for the docks, and it causes me to feel apprehension. When he disappears around the corner, I hurry back to join the two women. I must have truly not been paying attention earlier, for when I come back to stand beside them, my mouth falls open in astonishment. I end up gasping instead of speaking, and my shock causes a worried look to come to both of their faces.

"You're sisters," I breathe out, stating the obvious.

I am so dumbfounded by what I am seeing that I cannot help but say it aloud. I had never seen identical twins in my whole life, and it takes a moment for me to accept what my eyes are seeing. If they had been dressed exactly the same, I would not have been able to tell them apart.

"It is not safe here," I begin again, stating the obvious a second time, "and we need to get away from here. My name is Zeke of Dumnonia, and I would be honored to escort you to wherever you would like to go."

Glancing at each other with what seemed to be a shared grin despite the circumstances; Ruby is the first to speak up.

"We have nowhere to go, Zeke. That is why we are here in this alley in the first place. We have been trying to seek passage on a ship for days now, but have yet to find a ship's captain willing to take two unescorted females aboard their ship."

I digest this news unhappily, trying to think of what to do, and knowing I had better think of something quick. When the bells begin to toll from new sections of the city, I do not grasp at the implication of their meaning.

Too many things have been happening in these last few days, and my thoughts are in a state of confusion. Damn my luck to Hell, I curse silently. What in the hell is going on? The incessant ringing is not helping matters, and it dawns on me that the sound is erupting in too many places. Could there be that many fires in the city? Then I hear the deep rhythmic booming bass of bells, mixing with the higher-pitched clamoring of the fire bells, and I realize what is happening. The city is under attack!

The implications of what this means spurs me into action.

"Come! There is no time for questions. Just trust me."

My tone of voice leaves no room for argument, and without hesitation they begin to follow me down the alley.

"Wait!" Ruby calls out.

I turn; about to admonish them about the delay, but instead, I wait anxiously as they quickly pull their possessions from where they had hidden them behind some crates. Keeping to the shadows, and hoping I can get us safely to the shack without further incident, I lead them through the streets.

People begin to flood the streets, confused, and frightened. Most are in their nightclothes; hanging on to bleary eyed children as they shout questions to their neighbors, and stare at the sky. The disorder makes it difficult for us to make progress, but easier for us to go unnoticed by anyone looking for me. It seems like hours before we make it to the shack, but my luck has returned to me, and we make it back without a single confrontation.

Ruby and Sapphire look about the small shack with trepidation as I light some candles, and then the fireplace.

"It's not much, but it's safe," I venture in an attempt to ease the tension.

"Its fine," Ruby replies as she tosses her pack into a corner, and leans a staff she had been carrying against the wall beside it, "it's better than sleeping in an alley."

"My thoughts exactly," I say with a grin. "You two make yourselves at home."

My nervousness is apparent, and I cannot help but wonder what Able will think when he walks in the door.

They seat themselves at the table, and I can tell they feel out of kilter as I fill a large pot with water from a storage barrel beside the fireplace.

"I imagine you will want to clean up, so I'll heat this up for you to use for that purpose."

The words cause Sapphire to begin sobbing. Vexed, it hits me as to the reason why as I hang the pot over the fire. The thought of cleaning herself up after what has happened to her has refreshed the incident in her mind. Damn.

Other matters need immediate attention, and the incessant tolling of the bells demand that I try to find out what the situation is. The bells can mean we are still in danger from whoever is attacking the city, especially if they have breached the city walls. Still annoyed at myself, and using this as an excuse to leave the shack so they can have some privacy, I take my leave of them.

When I return, it is an hour before midnight. I find the girls to be a bit anxious, but in much better spirits. Able has not returned yet, and though the fire bells are still tolling, the attack bells have fallen silent.

I inform the girls of what I have been able to find out as we sit around the table.

"There wasn't an attack. In gathering information, the most reliable news I overheard came when a group of guards addressed a group of citizens in the street. They claim that agents of the elves have infiltrated the city. The agents have sabotaged the water supply, burned warehouses and ships, and destroyed other vital resources that the city needs to survive an attack or a siege. The city is crippled, and I'm willing to bet it's just a matter of days before they do attack the city in full force, if not sooner."

"Then we must flee here immediately," Sapphire gasps.

"But how can we?" Ruby counters, twisting her fiery red hair worriedly.

My thoughts are straying as I look at the two of them. They had to tell me, who is who, when I returned because they had changed into clean robes that are as indistinguishable as they are. Even their voices sound the same, melodic, with a hint of brogue that gives away their Celtic lineage.

I find their faces quite attractive, and I study them as they speak. Their complexions are milky white, with a light dotting of freckles across the bridge of their noses. Their eyes are pale green, like a ripe green apple, and they mesmerize me. They both wear their bright red hair untamed, and it hangs in ringlets to just below their waist. I guess their age to be about the same as mine, or perhaps a year younger. I speak up when the discussion again turns to talk about fleeing the city.

"That's what Able and I was planning to do this very night, before we saved you from those men."

I blanch, remembering I should avoid that topic. Sapphire sees my discomfort, and is about to say something, but the door opens and Able strolls in. Thanking the Gods for his timing, I turn to greet him. His astonishment at seeing the girls sitting with me at the table equals that which I had been anticipating. He nearly faints.

Our laughter at his expression makes him get a grip on himself, and he joins us at the table. The girls take this moment to thank us both profusely for their rescue, much to our chagrin, and Able quickly changes the subject.

CHAPTER NINE

Flight to Freedom

As we talk about the table, we find out that Ruby and Sapphire are also on the run, and dodging the authorities. They had lost their mother a few years ago when a jealous lover stabbed her to death during a quarrel. Fortunately, a kindly old man, who had been a longtime friend of their mothers, saved them from the city orphanage by taking them in.

Unfortunately, their new guardian died peacefully in his sleep a few weeks back, thus leaving the girls to deal with affluent family members who were not so inclined on finishing the two girls' upbringing. Threatened again with placement into an orphanage, the girls ran away, hoping to board a ship to Mildenheath, and seek help from another family friend who had opened a trading outpost there a few months ago.

"All we need to do is get onboard a ship to Mildenheath," Ruby states forlornly.

"Mildenheath is now in the hands of the elves. I fear your friend may have perished in the attack. It is said that atrocities were committed by the elves that left no man, woman, or child alive, and that none who were in the settlement had been able to flee their wrath," Able says, letting the news sink in, and not liking having to tell them what he knows.

The girls look glum, but one has to admire their spunk for at least trying to escape the city on their own. The sudden silence makes everyone look at each other expectantly, and listen into the night. It is right at the midnight hour, and the bells have stopped their tolling. Able gets up to go look out the window.

I join him by the window a moment later, needing the opportunity to talk quietly with him away from the girls. The sky looks eerie and thick clouds of smoke hang over the city, blocking out the stars above. Hesitantly, and expecting Able to outright laugh at the absurdity of the suggestion, I put forth what I have been thinking.

"If they will accept, can't we offer to take them along with us?"

Complete silence follows the question. I stand uncomfortably beside him as he pulls out his pipe, and begins chewing thoughtfully on the stem.

"I cannot think of any other way to help them, nor am I inclined to leave them to fend for themselves, Zeke. It goes against the code of chivalry to do anything but ensure their safety, and see to their care."

"Able, you again surprise me. I didn't realize you were so honorable," I joke.

"I have my moments," he says after poking me in the ribs with the pipe stem. "Look, this poses to add difficulties to our plans that you might not understand, Zeke. Sneaking two of us across hostile territory, though difficult, can be done, but trying to sneak four, with three of you being green at that, may be suicidal. Our chances of making it to Lakenhall will be less likely. I have been weighing in my mind, which is worse; leaving them here in a city that might fall into the hands of the elves, or taking them with us to endure the hardships that we will face on the journey ahead. I think their survival chances would be better with us, of course, but that'll be up to them to decide for themselves."

We return to the table, and put forth our ideas to the girls. Able retells the story he had told me, and then offers them the same proposal. To allow them some time to discuss the matter in private, Able and I take leave of them.

We step outside, close the door, and sit upon the ground with our backs leaning against the weathered planks of the shack. The night is too quiet, and the light no longer brightens the sky from the fires. In the darkness, we quietly discuss what we should do if the girls choose to come with us. It is nearly an hour before they join us. They come out bearing glasses of wine, and a small platter of sweetmeats and cheese.

Able offers up a toast to the success of our expedition when they inform us that they have decided to accompany us on the long journey. We supped; each lost in our own thoughts, and sipped on the cheap tart wine.

"I know everyone is tired," Able comments, noticing the yawns that the lateness of the hour provokes, "but we must stay up for a few more hours, and sleep during the day. This will better prepare us to deal with traveling the night through. I cannot express how important it will be for you to obey my every command without hesitation, for your life may very well depend on it, and I will not accept anything less if I am to get us there safely."

Everyone nods their acceptance of Able's request, thus bestowing upon his shoulders the responsibility of being the leader of the group. The following evening, as we prepare for our departure, a herald, accompanied by a group of guards, stops just outside the shack. The guards begin going door to door urging all the residents to gather in the street at the king's request.

Ruby steps outside while we hide quietly within the shack. The herald, richly garbed, and somewhat out of sorts with having to perform his job in such a poor, underprivileged area, waits impatiently for the last of the stragglers to gather about before he unrolls a scroll, and begins to speak in a nasally voice.

"Hear ye, Hear ye. It is with gode tidings from his majesty that I greet thee, and upon his orders that I must inform thee that not all is well. The city, as ye may very well know already, is preparing against the possibility of invasion by the alleged and self-proclaimed king of the elves. Every man above the age of fifteen is to serve in his majesties forces in defense of the city. Those who meet this condition are to gather in the field by the main gate at first light. You will receive

amazon.com

Returns Are Easy!

.... within 30 days for a full refund (other restriction's apply). Please have your order ID ready.

Your order of December 31, 2011 (Order ID 104-7241811-5809063)

Qty.	Item	Item Price	Total
1	**Mortal Conquests of the Dark Ages: The Wayfarers** Paperback (** P-2-D171C13 **) 1432771434	$11.57	$11.57

This shipment completes your order.

Have feedback on how we packaged your order? Tell us at www.amazon.com/packaging.

Subtotal	$11.57
Shipping & Handling	$3.99
Order Total	$15.56
Paid via credit/debit	$15.56
Balance due	$0.00

B2A

21/DTmk8vCTN/-1 of 1/1S/std-n-us/4019138/0106-19:00/0105-21:21/mengland

further instructions at that time. The king has ordered that no one will leave or enter the city until further notice. Desertion will be met with stiff penalties, and will also be considered an act of treason against the crown."

Shouted questions bombard the herald as he rolls up the scroll. The guards restore order with a few shouted commands, and menacing looks. The herald does take a moment to answer a few questions, but the guards soon insist that he must move on to notify the rest of the city's populace. Those gathered about linger for a short while discussing the news, but due to the lateness of the hour, most decide that a little rest before first light will serve them better than arguing about something they have little to no information about.

Ruby comes back inside, and fills us in on what we could not hear over the noisy crowd. When she finishes, I can tell Able is worried at the news.

"Our difficulties seem to be mounting," he states as we gather our gear. "May the Gods show favor upon us this night."

Solemnly, we ease into the quiet streets, and make our way to where Able's friend, Ruith, has hid the boat. We arrive without incident to find the boat, and Able's anxious friend waiting for our arrival.

We quickly board, stow our gear, and wait as Able and Ruith quietly discuss how to get us out of the harbor. When all is decided, Ruith and Able begin rowing, dipping the oars gently to prevent noise. The air smells of rain, and thick clouds thankfully hide the moon. The first flash of lightening illuminates the boat causing us great alarm. Thunder booms, and torrents of heavy rain begins to fall immediately after it rolls off across the water. We become miserably soaked, but thankful for the obscuring cover the rain provides.

The rain is so heavy at times that we have to bale water. It seems like we travel the night through, but it has been no more than a couple of hours before a hard grounding of the boat informs us we have made it to the shore. The flickering lightening shows us that we have landed on a rocky and steep bank.

At Able's bidding, I leap from the boat to pull it to higher ground. The girls gather their belongings, and join me on the bank, neither voicing a word of complaint at the miserable conditions. Able tosses out the rest of our gear, and bids his friend a somber farewell.

We have rowed a good distance east of the city. In fact, we cannot even see anything of the city anymore. Thunder rumbles as we climb the steep rocky bank, and crest the rise that brings us to safer ground. At Able's bidding, we take shelter under the branches of some scraggly trees, but it doesn't stop the rain from pounding down upon our heads.

"As we discussed earlier," Able reminds us, having to shout for us to hear him over the storm, "Zeke, you're in the rear. Girls, keep together between us, but spread out far enough to allow us swinging room should danger present itself."

Able hands each of the girls a dagger.

"Wait here a moment," Able bids, and then walks a short distance away.

When he returns, he's carrying a stout walking stick which he hands to Sapphire.

"Let's go," Able shouts as he slings his pack higher up on his shoulders, and looks back to assure everyone else is ready.

We journey northeast through dense brush, muddy fields, and the relentless rain, so the going is rough for the first few hours. Our goal, this first night, is to put as much distance as we can between us, and Haven's Rest.

When we come upon a rutted road, it is easier to walk along the side of it, rather than to sink knee deep in mud by walking upon it. Near dawn, Able finally gives in to our weariness, and enters a pine tree forest that borders a road that goes to St. Austell. He takes us well into the forest, and does not stop until he is sure our fire will not be easily seen should anyone pass by.

MORTAL CONQUESTS OF THE DARK AGES

The rain subsides to a drizzle by the time he finds a place he feels is fitting for a campsite. It is in a small clearing next to a swift moving stream that cuts through the forest. Stopping, he drops his pack, and signals that this is where we shall rest.

CHAPTER TEN
Sybal

Sybal had been following the man for months, all the way from Mildenheath, and deep into enemy territory. She was running out of time, and needed to kill the man soon. His death would help her to attain the position she most coveted from her cousin Zakinis, the new self-crowned king of the elves.

The man she followed was an emissary of King Custennyn, an impudent king whose actions or lack thereof, had provoked the elves into war with Dumnonia. In fact, the elves were about to declare war on several other human kings that were allowing their subjects to encroach upon the borders of Wynelvenest. The agent she was tracking was named Seth, a prominent representative of King Custennyn, and one her cousin also believed to be a spy.

She had been following Seth for several weeks now, and he was proving himself to be a worthy foe. The man was obviously no stranger to danger, and as the miles lengthened, he had given her no opening in which to send her poisoned arrow into his black heart. In fact, he had led her on an erratic return course that had her quite puzzled.

His meanderings had been so inconsistent, that she was wondering if he suspected that someone was following him. She could not allow him to reach Caer-Uisc, the capital of Dumnonia, where his king was now in residence. Now that the elves had declared war, she was especially vulnerable, being that she was an elf deep within enemy lines. She had taken great care to disguise herself as a human boy, but even that had its complications.

The ship that had brought her a good part of the way into enemy terrain had almost not granted her passage because the ship's captain had thought she was a runaway, or worse. Using her boyish charm, and a laden coin pouch, she was able to change his mind. This was a good thing for her, since it had saved her the embarrassment of losing her prey.

Though Seth's course had been strange, she was now certain he was heading towards Caer-Uisc. She had only a few days before he would reach the city, so she would have to strike at him soon. It was crucial that she stop whatever message he now carried, for if the message got through to his king, it could change the balance of the war. To make matters worse, she knew an agent of her untrusting cousin had been sent to follow her, and that whoever the man was, he had cost her a chance to fulfill her duty. Sybal was probably the best assassin in Zakinis's stable, if not the very best, and she had known she was being followed within a half day's walk of leaving her cousins side at Mildenheath. Zakinis's distrust upset her, yet she could not blame him for wanting to keep an eye on those who were the closest to him.

That had not stopped her from sinking her arrow into the idiot a few moments ago, when he had compromised her mission. The dolt had assumed she was abandoning her quarry, mistaking her backtracking as a sign that she had given up on her mission. The mistake had cost him his life. Kneeling down, she pulls back the man's hood to reveal his face, confirming her suspicion that it is Lewyl of House Dy'Palyn, an assassin of great renown, and a close friend of her dear cousin. A warm satisfaction fills her, not because she has taken down someone of his ability, but because she has just moved up a notch on her esteemed cousin's ladder.

Placing a boot on his chest, Sybal pulls the shaft out and inspects it to make sure the tip is still attached. She then pulls a dagger from one of the many spots where she keeps them hidden, aligns the tip, and plunges the black blade into the hole left by the arrows removal. Twisting it several times, the dagger enlarges the hole sufficiently, making it impossible to tell that an arrow had done the dirty deed. This was a precaution she took to make it impossible for anyone finding the body to discern that an elves arrow had killed the man. Wanting to make it look like a robbery by highwayman, Sybal takes everything of value from the corpse, and departs.

She begins following Seth's trail anew, silently cursing the fool Lewyl for merely wounding the man, and not killing him outright. Stopping a few miles from where she had left Lewyl's body, Sybal carefully buries all the valuables she has taken from the body. It will not go well for her should any of Lewyl's possessions be discovered on her. It upset her to have to bury the man's beautiful bow, but it was a necessary loss. Adding his coins to her pouch, she surveys her handiwork, and resumes the hunt for her wounded quarry.

Studying the tracks, she discerns that Seth's footsteps are faltering, and that he will have to stop to dress his wound or keel over from the loss of blood. She can only hope that Lewyl had poisoned the tip of his arrow, thus making her job that much easier. As she continues to track the man southeast, Sybal begins warring with her conscience as she recalls the last several months following her cousin's ascension.

Zakinis's takeover had been brutal. He had not only stripped the former governing council nobles of power, but he had also seen to it that the heads of those who had opposed him had been put up on pikes before the city gates of Ce'Annabreece. This gave testimony to their new king's tolerance for those who chose to remain in defiance of his authority. Sybal had been careful to align herself quickly with her cousin by requesting to accompany Zakinis on his first campaign that started with the conquering of the Draabitz Isles.

Upon their arrival, Zakinis proved he was in no mood to show mercy to the piratical halfling nation. The elves fast fleet of warships had decimated the halflings slower fleet of plunder ships in less than a week, and the impudent raiding of the elves coastline by the halflings ended abruptly. Within a month, Zakinis had forced the halflings into submission.

A short respite had followed the takeover of the Draabitz Isles, for Zakinis had needed to return to Wynelvenest to visit a band of gnomes. In exchange for the gnome's innovative expertise, and his promise to protect them, Zakinis had given the gnomes permission to settle within the elves borders. The new alliance made Zakinis a formidable force, for he now had at his disposal some of the gnome's greatest inventions.

The gnomes were providing Zakinis with war machines, and assault ships that were far superior to any other nations. Her cousin had been quick to manipulate the greedy little gnomes by using trinkets and baubles to entice them into mass-producing the inventions for his armies. Her cousin's obsession to rule, and the force he intended to use to subdue those who thwarted him had frightened her. His viciousness had become even more apparent as she witnessed the sacking of Mildenheath. She was a killer, but somewhere in her mind she had drawn a line, and followed a code of ethics where killing was concerned. What she had witnessed at Mildenheath had crossed, and conflicted with her code of ethics. Zakinis's ruthlessness had mortified her, and shaken her faith in him.

At Mildenheath, Zakinis had not only allowed his men to kill all the menfolk, but he also let the men mutilate the corpses beyond recognition. Further atrocities came by his hand when he allowed the defiling of the settlement's women before slaughtering them like cattle in a pen. The worst illustration of his cruelty, perhaps because she was a woman, had come when he had required the children to watch the killings, before hanging them by their necks above the burning doorsteps of their former homes. These acts spoke volumes into Zakinis's mindset, and she knew she had to walk a fine line where the man was concerned.

It did not help that Zakinis was seriously infatuated with her, and that he was growing bolder with his subtle attempts to swoon her into his bed. His hinting left no doubt in her mind that he intended on making her his queen. Though she wanted power, she did not intend to bed her cousin, or any other man for that matter. Zakinis did not suspect her loathing, but the longer she rejected his interests, the harder it was becoming. Now that he was in power, there was nothing to keep him from pushing the issue, so she had leapt at the chance to go on this mission, and get away from him for a while. Regrettably, she sensed that the end of the mission was neigh at hand, and though she dreaded having to return to him, there was really no other choice.

Breaking her reverie, Sybal draws up sharply, realizing her senses had proven true. The crumpled form of the spy lay up ahead in the road. Swiftly leaving the road, Sybal begins to move silently from tree to tree, her bow coming instinctively to her hand, while her other hand slips an arrow from her quiver.

The forest to each side of the road is acting like a funnel for a strong breeze, which is blowing directly at the back of her prey. This is good, because this will lend greater force to the missile when it strikes him. Sybal works her way into easy range, and to a point where her view is unobstructed. Satisfied, she notches her bow, and begins to draw.

Before she can pull the string to her cheek, movement in the forest across the road causes her to pause.

"Father?" she hears the boy cry out as he runs from the tree line to kneel beside the injured man.

She can only look on angrily as three more people rush out from the trees to join him.

"Zeke," Seth asks hoarsely in amazement.

"Yes, father," I moan.

Fighting to control the emotions choking me, I cradle my father's head, and pour water into his mouth from my waterskin. In dismay, I stare at the arrow protruding from his back. His glazed eyes try to focus, and he chokes on the water I try to get him to drink. When I reach for the arrow, thinking to pull it out, Able seizes my hand to prevent me from doing it.

"The wound appears to be mortal, Zeke, and he'll surely die the faster if you pull the arrow free," Able states gently, his face showing the sorrow he feels as he looks at me.

Grasping my arm, my father peers into my eyes, and tries his best to speak.

His voice is nearly inaudible, and I have to lean close to understand his words.

"My son, is it truly you? I fear your man is right, boy, I am done for. I darest say the poison on the arrow has progressed within me beyond that which any healing potion can cure. I need divine healing, and I'm sure that this will not occur before the poison kills me."

I was able to talk with him for a few more minutes before he succumbed to death, and began his journey to the netherworld. His dying words had left me feeling encouraged, and most importantly of all, he had supported my decision to go on with Able to Canaan.

Able and I quietly dig a shallow grave in a nearby meadow while the twins fashioned a crude marker. After placing stones upon the mound to thwart wild animals from digging him up, we stood around his grave respectfully. I played softly upon his harp, a gift to me just before he passed away, and one that I will cherish for the rest of my days.

Able, wanting to give me some time to mourn his passing, allows that we would not continue our travels this day. I was thankful for the gesture, and my respect for Able grew tenfold.

CHAPTER ELEVEN
Do Unto Others

For three days, Sybal tracked them, unsure if she should kill them all, or return now that her mission was complete. They were proceeding in the general direction in which she had to return, so she decided it might be wise to learn their intentions.

She easily sneaked past the robed woman who stood guard that night, intent on overhearing whatever they would talk about by their campfire. What she heard was enough to make her blood boil, and to want to kill the leader of their party for what he was planning.

She still seethed at what the arrogant halfling, Able, had said that night regarding his skills. He had asserted confidently that he could see their party cross Wynelvenest undetected. She would see about that. Without him to lead, she was certain the three humans would turn back immediately, and not dare to continue their journey.

The following day, Sybal carefully surveyed a spot from which to ambush their party. It was perfect. A creek bed with large boulders, affording her a place to fire from cover and not be seen. Once her arrow claimed the halflings life, she would then vanish without a trace by using the rocky bed of the stream beside her to hide her tracks. Her patience was steadfast, and before long, she heard the sound of their approach. Before she could notch an arrow, something stung her leg.

Screaming in agony, she jerks her leg away from the bite of a serpent she had failed to notice in the rocks. Before the snake can strike again, her foot slips on a mossy rock, and she finds herself plunging head first into the shallow water of the creek.

Sybal can feel the lethal venom racing up her leg as the icy water rushes over her body. She can feel hot blood running freely down her neck, where her head must have stuck a rock during the fall. Struggling to remain conscious, she feels hands seize her, and begin to drag her from the water.

"Whoa now," Able exclaims as the groggy elf woman draws forth a dagger, "we are friendly despite that which is transpiring between our nations. Please, we only wish to help."

Sybal knows that if she does not let them help, she might not have the strength to address her injuries. Shivering, she forces herself to swallow her pride, and put away her dagger.

"I've been snake bit," she says in elfish, forgetting that they might not understand her language.

The puzzlement in their faces makes her repeat what she said again in halfling, since she is terrible at speaking the rough guttural language that the humans speak.

Able bends to examine the bite once she exposes the wound.

"Here, drink this," he says as he removes a stopper from a vial he takes from his pack.

Sybal, too weak to take the vial from his hand, allows him to cradle her head, and pour the bittersweet liquid into her mouth. She barely manages to swallow it before she passes out.

"Are you sure she won't try to kill us in our sleep?" Ruby asks of Able, having detected earlier the hatred in the elf woman who is now slumbering peacefully in her tent.

Sapphire, who is sitting beside the elf, looks up anxiously, but Able smiles reassuringly.

"I assure you she will not forsake our kindness by doing that. Even the worst of the lot have deep-rooted codes of honor that would ensure me that she will not harm us while she is accepting our care. That does not mean she will not hesitate to do us mischief once she departs."

Sapphire had never seen a female elf in all her lifetime, and while the elf succumbs to slumber, she gazes upon the woman's beautiful features. She cannot help but wonder if she is actually seeing a goddess in mortal form, or some other spirited being from the legends and lore of old.

The elf woman must have clipped her ebony hair short to disguise herself as a young lad, and its spiky look helps to highlight the woman's faultless profile. Remembering how the woman's eyes had been a startling deep green, Sapphire shivers, for she also recalls how the woman's eyes had frightened her. They had held the look of pure hatred.

Sapphire envies the manner of dress the woman is wearing. The garb accentuates the woman's body in a way that is appealing to the eye, yet shocking in its revelations of her curvaceous figure. She resists the urge to stroke the black leather garb to see if it is as supple as it appears. Instead, she soothes the woman's forehead with a dampened cloth, admiring the woman's thigh high boots, and marveling at the way they mold to the woman's legs like a second skin. Sapphire blushes readily when she realizes the woman is watching her.

Sybal, having seen Ruby, and now having studied Sapphire's face during the time the girl was studying her, grudgingly decides that the human twins are pretty. Sybal had never seen identical twins in her lifetime, for it is exceedingly rare for an elf woman to birth two offspring at once. At first, seeing them had been unsettling, but not as unsettling as the serious mistake she had made during her assassination attempt.

Now that she has accepted their kindness, code depicts that she at least be agreeable to the situation she now finds herself in, no matter what her personal feelings are towards the humans. They have probably saved her life, and for that, she is grateful.

"Sapphire," Sybal says to the girl, knowing she is correct.

"Yes," Sapphire acknowledges.

"Don't look so surprised. My senses are much more acute than your human ones, and though you may look the same, I'm capable of knowing who's who."

Sybal tries to keep the disdain she feels for the woman's race, and the accursed language, from entering her voice as she speaks, but Sapphire's face betrays the fact that she has not succeeded very well. In fact, Sapphire even flinches away in fear when Sybal makes a sudden move to sit up. Sybal can sense the fear in the girl, and hears the wavering in her voice when she speaks again.

"Why do you hate us so much? I have never understood why people judge other people by the actions of others of their kind. Is it not your king who has brought war to our country because of what, differences of opinion, and things that *I've* not had anything to do with, nor will I ever have a say in those things because I'm a female? We could be friends. I've nothing against you or your people or anyone else who means me no harm."

Sybal allows the girl to scold her, suddenly liking her spunk. The girl's fear of her is evident, but she has spoken her mind despite her fear, and broaches a subject of which Sybal is deeply passionate about. Sybal has devoted her life to proving she is as good as any man, and has resented the limitations that men put on women. Sapphire's feelings echo hers in those regards and despite the fact that it went against her upbringing, the girl's other opinions are quite logical too.

Centuries of imbedded resentment towards the human race cannot easily change her mind in one conversation, but Sapphire's words have hit a cord in her that leaves her questioning herself, and her perspectives. Do not the elves pride themselves in their ability to be open-minded, and objective? The girl's wisdom is beyond her years, and Sybal can find no fault in her reasoning.

"I am sorry. No harm will I bring thee, nor the others whom thee travel with, Sapphire. An elves word is solemn, and is not freely given. My name is Sybal, and I am indebted to thee for thy help. You speak of being friends. An elf takes friendship very seriously, as serious as the joining of a man and a woman, and the bond needed to form that union takes time and much effort."

Sapphire can tell that the strain of the conversation is tiring Sybal, and suggests the elf woman rest. Almost immediately, Sybal surrenders to sleep once more.

"I see you are feeling better," Able comments when he finds Sybal the next morning stooped over the fire.

Sybal pats out another small cake of dried berries, and rabbit meat before answering. Her lips form into a pout, and she rubs her stomach to add emphasis to her complaint.

"Wherever did you get that vile liquid? Granted it worked, but my insides have been torn up something fierce."

Chuckling, Able swipes a corner from a cake that is baking on a flat rock, and his reward is a stinging slap to his hand for the effort.

"You're quick," Able observes, somewhat annoyed that her reflexes had been faster than his, "bet you a copper you can't do that again."

His fingers smart from the stinging crack of the switch she has somehow managed to pick up and hit him with before he had even brushed the cake with his fingertips. Reluctantly, he digs a copper from his pouch.

"No need to mope about it," Sybal sniggers, suddenly reminded of his boasting by the fire the other night.

Sybal almost makes a huge mistake of mentioning the folly of their plans, but stops herself short before making such a grave error. They have no idea she had been spying on them. Stating her knowledge of their intentions to cross through Wynelvenest would have triggered questions, and caused suspicions to arise. She did not want to jeopardize their trust in her, especially if she could use that trust to her advantage.

"It's none of my business, but where are all of you going?"

Able's discomfort in her calculated question is evident, but he answers truthfully. She had not expected him to do that. Actually, she was counting on him to lie so she could renew her anger and resentment towards them. She did not like having the wind taken from her sails, or the fact that they were able to shake her belief that they were not as evil as the elders had taught her to believe.

"Surely you jest. You would never make it through Wynelvenest alive, unless Zakinis has granted permission to you of course, and besides that, you're talking about almost several months of travel inside enemy lines during very troubling times. In addition, your companions do not appear to be too fresh off their mother's nipple, judging from what I have seen so far. It would be foolish to attempt to travel so far with three inexperienced people."

Sybal knew well that they did not have permission to cross the border, but was waiting to see if Able would lie, and claim they'd been granted safe passage.

"Tis truth you speak. However, to be honest, and though I fear I should not be telling thee this, there is just no other way we can go. You must believe me when I say we would ask permission, but to whom do we ask, you? I doubt we can get audience with anyone in that position, so we are willing to take our chances. I am fully aware of why you are upset with the humans, and for that matter, why you are upset with the Draabitz. People have crossed your borders for centuries with impudence, never giving thought to asking permission. My people have been no different, yet I assure you that I have suffered deeply by their acts. Not all Draabitz accepted those who seized power, and we deeply resented when they chose to make the elves our enemies by raiding your lands. My family worked hard fishing the seas, and we minded our own business. Of late, the wealthy gained power, and forced the commoners into an existence that was no better than that of a slave. Your beliefs, in the earth being like a Mother, I have learned in my travels, but others have not."

Seeing that his words are making an impression, he hurries to say everything that is on his mind.

"People cross the land without respect for Mother's preservation, and Mother sometimes cannot repair the harm their crossings have caused her. I travel the land the way you do because I understand, and agree with your teachings. I am teaching these humans to do the same. I will do what you suggest, if there is hope of obtaining permission, but if not, we still must go through Wynelvenest. We cannot turn back, and I have plenty of time to teach them how to survive before we reach Wynelvenest. Is there any way you can help us?"

"Able, you have gnome in thee. Am I right?" Sybal asks, ignoring the question while trying to gain a little thinking time.

Not expecting the question, Able nods yes.

"You would be allowed to come and go as you please in Wynelvenest. If you do not know already, the Draabitz have come under our rule, and the gnomes are under our protection as well. The problem you face is in your association with the humans," Sybal relates.

"You will be attacked immediately, and tried for treason should you be found with them within our borders. It will be the same should I be found with thee in this land I suspect. Your silence will buy mine, though tis treasonous all the same. I will travel with thee until we reach the border. From there, you take your own chances."

Able accepts what Sybal says without further comment, hopeful that at least he might not have to worry about her giving them up once they cross into Wynelvenest. Something about the woman still worries him though. She has not ventured to reveal why she is so far from the safety of the elves. Is she a scout for an approaching army? Her bearings are not that of a soldier, though her weapons appear to have seen much use. He thinks to ask, but changes his mind.

When Able asks if she needs more time to rest, Sybal insists that she is well enough to travel, so they decide to go on. Able packs his gear, but his thoughts still harangue him. Where do Sybal's loyalties lie? Puzzled, Able watches as she helps break down the camp. She is dexterous, not wasteful of movement, and she reminds him of... himself? Perhaps she is a spy, or an agent of the elves army, sent on a mission to cause problems within the kingdom. One of the three makes sense, and if she is of any of those professions, can he trust her word?

He hadn't been born a fool, and he knew better to trust Sybal enough to let his guard down. If for a moment he started to think she would cause anyone in his adventuring group harm, he would not hesitate to take her out.

CHAPTER TWELVE
Sybal's Quandary

Three days of journeying finds us walking northeast through an ever changing landscape of moors, farmland, and wildflower fields. The road takes us south towards the rocky seashore, and then winds its way along the sea for a short while, before heading back inland in a northeasterly direction.

We leave behind the vistas of rock overlooking the sea, and begin to travel right through the more densely inhabited areas of the region. This becomes a time consuming process for a group of travelers not wishing to encounter anyone.

Many times, we have to leave the road, hiding from merchant wagons, roving military patrols, and the locals. The towns and villages we come across impede our progress, and sometimes force us to take real long detours to get around them. We avoid all contact with people, not because Able and I still fear capture, but because we fear for the safety of Sybal.

Able feels it is very doubtful that news of our crimes has traveled this far from Haven's Rest, but with Sybal in our group, our own safety is now in jeopardy. The further inland the road penetrates, the slower our progress becomes and twice we seek immediate cover as groups of knight's whisk by us on war steeds. The knights are probably heading towards the border to bolster the defenses of the outposts along it.

Within a few hours, we have three such encounters that find us diving into the brambles with not a moment to spare. When the knights are gone and the dust has settled, we ease our way out of the thicket. Exasperated, Able decides to reconsider the route we are taking.

"Hey, we can't keep going on this way, and not expect to run into someone. I hate to leave this road, but I fear we must. This is the only road that runs clear to the border, but it has become much more populated since I had traveled it years ago, and with war impending, I expect we will have many more encounters with the king's military. Sybal, do you know of another way?"

Sybal shakes her head no. "I've never been across the border before, taking this road. I'm afraid I'm unfamiliar with any other way of reaching the border."

Able digests the news, and we can tell he doesn't like the decision he is being forced to make. Besides, Sybal's statement makes him again wonder what business would bring her across the border, and just how she had gotten here in the first place. There was time to worry about the latter later, and he forces his mind to come up with a plan for their current problem.

Digging into his pack, he brings forth his most prized possession. It is a map of the islands, beautifully drawn, but lacking in detail because it is very old. He spreads the map out carefully on the ground, and points to the largest of the isles. He then uses his finger to show them where they are in relation to where they need to go.

"The Celts call these the Pretanic Islands. Their homeland of *ens hiernorum* or Ierne is to the west. Ierne is most probably the origin of your ancestors," Able comments, nodding his head towards the twins.

"The isle we travel upon is most commonly called Britannia, but it has other names as well. In order to get to Canaan, we will cross many kingdoms before reaching Hadrian's Wall, which is near Caer Ligualid in Rheged. King Meirchion Gul the Lean rules Rheged, and his kingdom is the largest one we must cross," Able explains, before pointing to another place on the map with his finger.

"At the northern tip of his kingdom, Emperor Hadrian built a wall to keep the barbarians at bay. I understand the wall runs nearly the breadth of the island, but it should not be a problem to cross because only a few soldiers maintain it anymore, unlike when the Romans maintained it," Able says, before moving his finger to another location.

"North of the wall, we find Wynelvenest. Head north further and you find the mountains of the dwarves. Further still, is where Canaan lies. North of Canaan is Caledonia, or sometimes I have heard it called Pictland, but that is all I know of it since I have never been there. What I do know, is that beyond Hadrian's Wall, you will find some of the fiercest beings on this isle." Able stops his narrative long enough to sip from his waterskin before he continues.

"Many creatures, including some of the lesser civilized races, are kept at bay beyond the wall because they are deemed too barbaric, and dangerous for civilized man to live with peacefully. As mortals expand, some races and creatures have been nearly wiped out of existence. It is very rare indeed to even see a dragon, an ogre, a dwarf, or even an elf below the wall anymore."

Sybal nods her head in agreement, but seems a bit miffed that Able dares infer that the humans would think that elves and dwarves were barbaric, and uncivilized.

Unnoticing, Able continues his narrative of the map. "To the east, fanned out along the eastern coastline, are the kingdoms of the Anglos, Jutes, Fresians, and the Saxons. Most refer to the middle of the island as the wilds, and through the years, one ruler or another has tried to lay claim to parts of this region, but none have been strong enough to root out the barbaric races that refuse to flee north across Hadrian's Wall. Therefore, few humans will risk trying to settle there. My friends, I do not like it, but this is where I intend to take us. I believe we stand a better chance if we go east into the wilds, and then try to go north"

Able lets them study the map a moment before stating what is bothering him.

"I must warn thee in advance, before we decide upon this course of action, that the wilds are a mysteriously perilous place. It is much like the lands north of the wall because there are still ferocious creatures which did not flee north before Hadrian built the wall. The wilds, and those creatures within it, are slowly feeling the squeeze as both the eastern and the western coastal populations expand inward. It will be an extremely dangerous journey should we go this way, for we will find not one friend there."

Suddenly realizing what Able is saying, I venture forth a question as I watch Sapphire, Ruby, and Sybal's reaction.

"So, if I am to understand what you imply, not only will the elves cause us harm, but we will be in mortal danger from other creatures once we cross Hadrian's Wall?"

Sybal interrupts before Able can answer.

"Aye, many of these creatures find sanctuary in our land, as well as in the land of the dwarves. Your lives are forfeit if an elf should come upon you within Wynelvenest, and doubly so if you encounter any number of creatures who hate you humans for having forced them from their homelands."

Sybal privately gloats on the impact of her words, hoping that the words will sway them from their quest. Except for Able, fear clearly shows in the eyes of the others. She can see that the halfling is quite uncomfortable with her upsetting answer, for he seems to not like how his group reacts to her revelations.

"So, if we will be in so much danger when we cross over the wall," Ruby asks, "why would you want to tempt fate by traveling through the wilds? Would this not put us into even more danger before it is necessary?"

"I am not suggesting we go into the heart of the wilds. Nay, just enter within it enough to avoid the populated areas, and of course, the military patrols. If we are to make it to Lakenhall before winter, we must find a faster way. However, if you want to continue traveling as we have been, then so be it. Since we will soon not be able to use the roads, we will have to pass through wilderness of dense forests, rugged hills and mountains with deep valleys. Add peat moorlands, bogs, lakes, and the many streams that we will have to negotiate, and you can see why time becomes a concern. The terrain is not our only difficulty. There are many creatures in our path that will also try to prevent us from making it to Lakenhall by winter. To be fair, we shall vote on it," Able insists.

"I will trust your judgment Able," I decide. "My vote is for getting off this road and seeking the faster route."

Except for Sybal, all heads nod favorably for skirting the fringes of the wilds, and though he admires their confidence in his decision, Able feels a knot form in the pit of his stomach. Is he leading his sheep to slaughter?

"Sybal, I can understand your decision. I am sure I speak for all of us when I say that we will honor our oath to see you safely to your homeland, but should you decide that you must go your own way, we understand," Able admits, secretly hoping she will choose to leave.

"I must return to Wynelvenest quickly," Sybal admits, "and I think I must leave you. Returning to my homeland is imperative. I can get back faster by continuing upon the road. I hope you understand, and accept my thanks for having helped me in my time of need."

Her announcement causes a mixed reaction, but Sybal ignores the reaction, and begins gathering her belongings as Able continues to explain the route to us.

"According to my map, we should head towards Aquae Sulis, a place that is famous for a spring of hot water that comes from the ground, and where the Romans have built some bathhouses. I'm not sure if the town is still called that, or even if it is still there, due to the age of this map, but it is the best plan I can come up with," Able finishes explaining just at the moment Sybal returns to say her farewells.

Sybal says her goodbyes to a very mixed and emotional party, and then she departs without a backwards glance. All eyes watch her until she vanishes into the surrounding brush. Able breathes a sigh of relief, making sure the others do not see his reaction. Very happy that Sybal has chosen to leave, he continues making plans for their change in course. With nothing further to discuss, Able wastes no time getting them moving again.

"Fools", Sybal mutters, as she watches them from a hiding spot a short distance away. In a way, she had hoped they might suddenly change their minds and continue by way of the road, but they had not. Instead, they headed with purpose, straight northeast towards the wilds.

She had chosen to leave them because she knew the halfling favored it. Besides, she really did need to return with her report to Zakinis, but for some reason she had begun doubting her decision. She had gone no further than a few miles north when she came upon a realization that struck her like a blow from a club. At first, she could not believe what she was feeling, but by that evening, the emptiness became epidemic, and she could not quell the fact that she was missing Sapphire horribly.

Though the twins may have looked identical, their personalities were as different as night was from day. Sybal could tolerate Ruby, but she had little in common with the others. Sapphire was different, and seemed to understand her. Unlike anyone she had ever met before in her lifetime, Sapphire seemed to share much of her philosophies. In the little time she had been around Sapphire, their relationship had blossomed into a friendship akin to what the elves called "wiccalwa", or the merging.

Wiccalwa is an attraction between those of her race that is akin to what humans call love, but in a deeper, and more sacred way. Sybal wonders, as she wars with herself, if wiccalwa has ever occurred between an elf, and someone of another race. The question confounds her, as well as the unshakable feeling she is experiencing the further from Sapphire she travels. She tries to shake it off, but is unable to loosen its grip on her.

Shaken by what it could mean, she thinks she can sever the bond by putting even more miles between them, but it isn't long before she realizes that she cannot. A linking or bond with Sapphire had indeed formed. She knew this to be true when she began to feel the "deldra", or the separation, the further away from Sapphire she went.

Deldra is akin to what a dryad experiences when they are separated from their tree for too long. This separation can lead to the dryad's death, should one or the other perish or be separated for an extended period of time. She begins to wonder if Sapphire is experiencing what she is feeling. What if one or the other should perish, would deldra succumb to "lawtra"?

Lawtra occurs upon the death of one emotionally attached to another by Wiccalwa. This loss subjects the one who still lives to experience an emotional mourning period, or "lawtra". This could, if the bond had been for a lengthy period, lead to the death of the other. The two of them were not together long enough for this to occur, but still, she needs to know if what she is feeling is truly Wiccalwa.

Maybe she is the bigger fool, or maybe she still isn't too anxious to return to the pressures that being around Zakinis presents, but she has to know if Sapphire is feeling the same as she, so she turns around and returns to the last place she saw them.

She begins following their trail, hoping that it will not rain and wipe it out before she can rejoin them. It takes two days to backtrack them, and fortunately, the weather remains favorable. It is the evening of the second day, when she comes upon them making camp. Knowing that one would be on guard while they set up their camp, she calls out well before she can cause them alarm.

They greet her affably enough, though Able appears vexed. He hides it well from the others, but Sybal sees the flicker of irritation in his eyes when she appears. Sybal studies Sapphire's reaction to her return closely, but though her response is warm enough, it is not quite what she expects.

"I just couldn't let you go on without me. Not because I need you, mind you, but because I believe you need me."

Able cannot hide his facial expression, which appears to be like one who just bit into a sour grape. He is already suspicious as to why she has decided to return, but to imply that he is incompetent rattles him. He can feel anger well up inside him and then coldness as he forces himself to feel nothing. The coldness is a way to calm his anger when he is about to draw his daggers. He has learned to retain a state of lucidity when engaging in battle, and he never allows hot-headedness to blind him before a fight.

Sybal can see the transformation in Able's eyes, and hurries to explain when she realizes he has taken what she has said the wrong way. She knows she has hurt the halfling's feelings and has wounded his pride, but worst of all, she has questioned his leadership abilities. Her words are a subtle challenge, and she suspects that he will not let the challenge go unanswered.

"Please Able; forgive my rudeness and lack of forethought regarding my choice of words. I do not mean to challenge your authority, nor do I wish to insult you. I merely mean that I can assist you. I am not sure if you have thought about this, but these three are in sore need of education in many areas of survival, and definitely in the use of weapons. I simply want to help you improve their chances of making it to Canaan by assisting you in their instruction."

Mollified enough to stay his hands from drawing his daggers, but not appeased enough to trust her, he decides to tell her what is on his mind.

"I believe I speak the minds of all when I say this Sybal, and I trust that you will not be angered by our concerns. We know nothing about you, or your reasons for coming so far south of the wall. We suspect it is to cause mischief, in one way or another, in support of the war and thy cause. This concerns us not, and you know that we have done thee no harm, and have shown you nothing but respect. Our only concern is to succeed in our quest, and leave this land of constant feuding behind us," Able says, pausing a moment to think how to word what he wants to say without further offending the elf.

When Able continues, he speaks very carefully. "We do not seek refuge in your land, though we mean to cross through it because that is our only option. We welcome thee as a friend and ally, and hope we can trust you. I have thought about what you mentioned, and just last night, I began teaching them the basics of defense. Your help in this area would be most welcome and deeply appreciated. In a showing of good faith, we simply request that you give us your oath, and allegiance."

She knew that her return would cause this reaction, and having had two days to prepare her answer, she answers without hesitation.

"I understand thy concerns, Able, and they are justly raised. I harbor no ill will in their asking. It is true I was up to no good when I crossed the border, and if you will permit that to be enough said about it, I will give my oath, and allegiance to thee. Furthermore, I will hold to that oath until you are safely through Wynelvenest. Mind you, I have no authority to grant you safe passage, and I cannot guarantee I have enough influence to prevent your being killed should we come across elves or others who would do you harm. What you do not know is that I am the cousin of our new king, a king who loves me dearly. I am pretty sure I can petition his leniency where you are concerned should that become necessary."

Sybal's stunning news has the intended effect of deflating Able's anger, and though she suspects she has laid Able's suspicions to rest, she knows he is not one to trust her on her word alone. Able agrees not to press her further on what her business has been, and everyone votes favorably to accept her back into the party.

CHAPTER THIRTEEN

Teaching the Teachers a Lesson

When I play my father's harp, I feel it lending strength to me. It is as if his essence still lurks within the instrument. Spidery webs of his soul linger in the strings, vibrant, pulsing ripples, ebbing into me. Without that strength, I wonder if I can continue to go on each day.

I have had little time to immerse myself in melancholy since my father's passing. We do not just walk the daylight hours through, and waste the evening hours in our own idle pleasures anymore.

"You have made your bed now lay in it," were words of wisdom my mother had always said when I had made a decision that ended me up in lots of trouble.

I was just a snot nosed child then, trying to see how far I could test those words of wisdom, hoping that she would be wrong, but that was then, and this is now. I can no longer afford the luxury of learning a lesson the hard way, accept the punishment that follows, and go on to make the same mistake again. I am not a child anymore. Able and Sybal have clearly beaten that into my head these last few days. They say I may not live to make the same mistake twice, but I wonder at times, if I will just survive their lessons.

My mistakes have been many, and I have the welts to prove it, but I refuse to be beaten, and I meet the challenges of the next lesson with enthusiasm, though my body protests the abuse. Besides, I cannot allow myself to show discomfort when my learning rivals are two pretty woman who tenaciously try to outdo me.

I try to convince myself that Ruby and Sapphire are more distressed than I am from the additional toil these lessons have burdened our endurance with, but I am unable to find fulfillment in this because they refuse to show it. I awake each morning barely able to move, and as we break camp, they flutter about seemingly refreshed. It is irritating to see, but I have to admit they have grit.

We have welcomed the fair weather, and despite the ruggedness of the terrain, we have made excellent time. The road has become more like a trail used by wild animals, one minute it is there, and the next it completely disappears altogether. The last few hours finds us walking through meadows of grass so high, Sybal and Able can barely see over it. The day goes on, and as evening approaches, we enter into a clearing.

The clearing is as out of place as the stone that rests within its center. Clearing her throat, Sybal breaches the silence, and voices her concerns.

"I don't like this. It is my bet that there is some kind of protection spell encompassing this area. There are many holy places one should not tread upon within the realms, and though I have never laid eyes on one of these ancient sites, we elves have been taught to respect them as powerful places of magical importance," Sybal relates, looking at each of us beseechingly, hoping that for once we will heed her advice.

"Don't you think it's just a bit odd that this should be here, surrounded by a sea of grass, and in the middle of nowhere?" She adds quickly, hoping again that we will agree with her reasoning, and not step into the clearing. Everyone nods in agreement except for Able.

Able tries to keep a straight face, and not let his excitement show, but his imagination is running wild. He begins envisioning bolts of lightning searing the mortal who would dare enter the sanctuary of the leaning rocks shadow.

"Really, you think it could be magical? I mean, you are right of course. We should be very cautious. Here let me see if it's safe, I'll run, and check it out," Able hastens to add.

Before Sybal can protest further, Able takes off across the clearing.

Sybal looks at Zeke in dismay. "I cannot believe he just did that!"

Since I am familiar with Able's recklessness, I shake my head side to side speculatively before commenting, "Well, nothing's happened to him, yet."

We watch Able run in circles around the stone, not sure what we should expect to see happen to him if Sybal's assessment of the clearing proves to be the truth. Able hollers out elatedly as he comes back into view, and bangs his fist into the palm of his other hand to add emphasis to his evaluation of the area.

"See I didn't think anything would happen, it's just a big rock sticking out of the ground."

The rock is as large as a wagon stood on end, tilting to the point one would wonder not if, but when it will fall. Surrounding the stone is a 30-foot swath of cleared area, perfectly square, and equally unusual. The mysteriously cropped grass within the clearing is within inches of the ground, each blade precisely the same height as another, and one can only wonder whom, or what maintains it that way.

"We'll make camp here," Able proclaims, despite the alarmed look that appears on Sybal's face.

"Come on, nothing's going to happen." Able scoffs, trying to hide the excitement in his voice.

He looks at me, but I kept my face a mask as he tries to discern if I am thinking he has definitely lost his mind.

"I don't like it," Sybal restates with palpable concern in her voice.

A serious debate with Sybal follows, but Able wins out, his logic being that we have no idea how far the thick grass will continue, and if it does, would we be able to find a more suitable place to camp before nightfall? Still not liking it one bit, Sybal finally gives in to the majority.

As usual, I am the last to show up for our lessons this evening. Able and the twins have already begun doing exercises to warm up for what lies ahead and Sybal is preparing a fire to cook our supper.

Evening is the time of day that my body is beginning to dread, but as I discover new abilities I had not known I possessed, the aches and pains that follow the new lessons each night are tolerable. During the day, either Able or Sybal leads us while the other fills our heads with new knowledge of how to survive in the wilds, and survive the intricacies of noble court.

They teach us history, not solely history in regards to government, or politics, but the history of the land. We learn of plants, animals, and of beasts that we had believed were only fairy tales told to scare us as children. They assure us that they are not, and to add to our qualms, they make sure we understand that we stand a good chance of encountering some of these beings as we travel. Our knowledge of the land we walk has been quite lacking, and I find I enjoy these instructions as much as I do the lessons in arms.

It is Able's turn to instruct us tonight in weapons use. At least we no longer have to cook. That chore now alternates between Able and Sybal, the cook being the one who has taught us our lessons during the day as we travel. It is a wonder we eat at all, because instead of cooking, the cook is usually too bemusedly busy, watching our annihilation.

Tonight we will continue our lessons in defense, and though I am anxious to learn the more aggressive uses of my sword, both of our teachers insist that we must learn to defend ourselves before we can learn how to hit back. I think I am a fast learner, but each night when I crawl into bed with bruises on top of bruises, I understand why they stress the importance of protecting oneself.

We finish warming up, and Able chooses Ruby to instruct first. Sapphire and I must stand guard duty during Ruby's hour of instruction, or as we fondly call it, our hour of destruction, which usually ends with them having beaten the living hell out of us.

Able is especially vicious tonight, and Ruby suffers a severe beating from him while Sybal groans audibly. The groaning is not because she has burnt the meat, but because Able's staff just bounced off Ruby's head for the third time in that many minutes. Sybal just happens to be watching the lesson more than her cook pot.

I wince when Ruby's staff sags, and Able drives the tip of his staff into her exposed belly. Before she can even double over in agony, Able's staff arches around behind her legs in a movement so fast, my mouth drops open. It sweeps her off her feet so hard, that she nearly flips completely over.

With a grunt, she lands hard on her upper back, and tries to suck in some air. She is as game as any man is though, and before Able can pin her, she leaps to her feet. Unfortunately, she regains her feet with her back to her opponent, and Able capitalizes on her mistake by cracking the staff across her back with enough force to drive her face first into the grass.

With a cry of anger, Sapphire abandons her post and rushes over, clearly concerned about her sister's welfare. Angered, Able rebukes her for abandoning her station so heatedly, that she quickly hurries back to it. During the confrontation, I see Sybal slink off into the tall grass and disappear.

The reason becomes apparent within moments. Like a ghost, Sybal emerges from the grass and encircles Sapphire's throat with a piece of cord before Sapphire can even cry out. She keeps the noose tight until Sapphire nearly passes out. Sapphire slumps to the ground gasping for air by the time Sybal does let up, and without any regard for her, Sybal returns to the fire. The three of us learn the importance of guard duty this evening, and never again will we fail to take the responsibility lightly.

Unfortunately, it is my turn to stand the first watch after our lessons end, as I cannot yet enjoy any free time until my hour of duty has ended. I am not long there before Sapphire glumly approaches to relieve me, telling me that Able feels she needs to hone her abilities to guard us better by standing a double watch.

I am unable to contain my joy at the news, and Sapphire shoots me an evil look as I gladly flee the duty. Knowing it will be at least another half hour before Sybal will finish our meal preparations; I clean up, and decide to practice upon my father's harp. It is my favorite time of the evening, especially since I have a dreamy eyed fan in Ruby, who if not on guard duty, will dutifully listen to me play.

My thoughts are interrupted when Ruby approaches. I nod a greeting as she gingerly takes a seat across from me, and tries her best to hide her discomfort. It's obvious she's very sore from today's vicious engagement with Able, because she sticks her tongue out at me when I smirk at her. Out of the corner of my eye, I see Sybal throw a perfectly aimed dagger at Able's hand. The dagger sticks deeply into the coals of the fire, separating Able's hand from a potato cake he is trying to filch when he thinks her back is turned.

"Hey," Able cries out, jerking his hand away from the cake.

He gives Sybal a look of consternation, as if he is innocent of any guile, and pleads, "it looked like it was about to slide off into the coals."

Sybal wags a second dagger at him threateningly, and Able hurriedly slinks away empty handed. He makes his way over to us with a sheepish grin, and I begin to strum on my harp. Ruby and I are already chuckling, but we begin to laugh harder when Able begins to gingerly break a hot potato cake into equal amounts for us to share with him.

"Able Nimblefingers," Sybal cries out angrily, "you'd best be enjoying that one, because you'll nary get another."

Saddened by the decree, Able chews his portion of the cake slowly, savoring its flavor until the last smidgen is licked from his fingers. When darkness settles in for the night, I put up my harp, and try to frighten Ruby by telling her creepy stories I'd learned from my father. Though she hates when I do this just before she is to stand watch, she always listens. Sybal completes the meal a half hour after sunset. In a gesture of kindness for my laughing at Sapphire, I bring her a trencher full of food, denying my own meal until she has eaten. Sybal always generously divides the food, and despite her declarations, I notice that Able is joyously devouring a trencher full of potato cakes and fish stew while I wait for my share.

After cleaning and stowing away his feasting gear, Able belches out loudly before taking a seat by the fire. I have learned his habits well, and I am not disappointed to see him fill his pipe, and begin smoking it. He appears to be relaxed, and lost in thought, yet I can tell it is just pretend. Sybal and Sapphire retire to the twin's tent to talk, another habit that when time offers the two to be alone, is as predictable as Able's smoke after a meal. I sit down beside Able, but it isn't long before the fires warmth lulls me to sleep.

Bored, and with curiosity eating away at him, Able casts furtive glances at the stone. Typical of a halflings nature, he dearly wants to explore the area around the stone. There isn't a moon this night, and the stone looks ominous as shadows dance about it from the campfire's light.

Deciding it will not hurt to just walk around it again, yet not wanting to be too obvious about it, Able goes to his pack, and pretends to rummage through its contents for a moment. Ruby is slowly walking the perimeter of the clearing, and he waits until just the precise moment to make his move.

When he is certain nobody is looking, he slips into the shadows behind the stone, and waits. Warily alert for danger and prepared to react should anything begin to happen, Able reaches out and touches the rock. When nothing happens, he kneels at the base and begins feeling around it with his fingertips, hoping to find anything that will make the rock more interesting, but his searching fingers find nothing.

Knowing he has but moments to spare before Ruby comes back around; he pokes and prods at the stones surface. Suddenly, he feels both sides of his ribs being sharply poked. Figuring he must have triggered a trap, and too afraid to move or call out lest he be skewered, he remains motionless. The shadows looming over him are menacingly evil looking phantoms, dark, and foreboding. Where is Ruby, he wonders? He is just about to cry out the alarm and tempt fate by trying to leap away, when the shadows begin to laugh.

CHAPTER FOURTEEN
Faerie Folk

"Really Able, I didn't say a word to her," Zeke swears. "She quietly woke me when she spotted you hiding behind the rock. I have to give her all the credit, for she set up the taking of you like a field commander. It was her idea for me to sneak around the opposite side of the stone, and upon her signal, move in. It was also her idea to try and take you without a fight, though should you have moved in an aggressive manner, I fear the harm we would have done to you."

Zeke's compliment causes more color to show in Ruby's already flushed cheeks.

"I'm quite pleased to see our lessons are paying off, and though you've passed this test, be assured there will be many more like this one," Able claims, as he rubs at the sore spots where the sword and staff had bruised his ribs.

It is much easier for Able to accept that he's planned it all along, than it is for him to admit how petrified he was a moment ago. In just a few moments, he's convinced himself that testing them had truly been the real reason why he was behind the stone in the first place. Able allows that the only thing he is upset about is that he was caught. Sybal and Sapphire gather around the dying fire, curious as to what the commotion is all about. Able doesn't like the knowing look that Sybal shoots him once the story is retold, and to convince her further that it was a test, he begins scolding Zeke and Ruby for a mistake he says was made during the test.

"The one thing you forgot to do was warn the whole camp. You did not know if there were others lurking out there in the grass. Had there been, the situation may have turned out different," he asserts as if he is instructing them.

He painfully recalls that he was too frightened to warn the camp as well, and because of this, he keeps his words from sounding too harsh. Able's rebuke encourages Sybal to add her own two coppers worth of advice, and Able is relieved to see she isn't eying him suspiciously anymore.

"This is true. Always call out a warning to everyone in the camp when the camp is endangered, even if you will lose surprise. Able, that was indeed a very good test and is something we should have taught them from the start."

Immensely happy that things go his way, Able promptly forgets about the incident, and begins to bank the fire for the night.

"Sapphire, I want to show you something," Sybal says.

Nodding, she follows Sybal into her tent, and just as the flap closes behind them, the candle blows out unexpectedly. She senses a flicker of energy at that moment which is like the energy she feels when a spell has been cast near her.

"Sapphire, can you relight the candle please?"

Fumbling around for the holder in the dark, she finds it, and starts to leave the tent to get a brand from the fire.

"Oh please Sapphire, who are you trying to fool, light the thing already. I know you can. You reek of feral magic."

She isn't sure what stuns her more, Sybal's ability to sense that she is able to use magic, or the fact that she is able to tell that she is a primitivist, or one who's able to use magic naturally from birth. Waving her hand, she lights the candle without more than a mere flicker of thought. Sybal simply smiles, and begins rummaging through her pack to find what she wants to show Sapphire.

Feeling the need to justify herself, she tells Sybal some things about her past.

"My mother had been born a primitivist, but we hadn't known of her ability until I accidentally set fire to our bed during a heated argument with my sister one night. Trapped by the fire, and mortified by what I'd done, my mother's casual extinguishing of the inferno had left us even more wordless than before. She hadn't needed an explanation, nor had she been angry. She'd been able to sense the powerful surge of energy and surmise instantly that one of us had finally demonstrated that we possessed her ability. Since we hadn't showed any ability to use magic since birth, our mother preferred to keep her ability a secret from everyone, including us, out of fear of what could happen if the wrong people were to find out.

In our society, a primitivist is as much feared as a roaming halfling in a marketplace, and those who possess the ability have suffered greatly at the hands of the Roman church. Since we were very late in showing our ability, which usually shows itself in early childhood, our mother had assumed her ability hadn't been passed on to us. She also felt that we were too young to be trusted with her secret. The next five years, before she was brutally murdered, she helped us explore our abilities. She told us that the fire was a lesson we should never forget, especially when we begin to have children of our own, for an untrained primitivist was as much a danger to themselves as they were to others.

Well, immediately following that incident, she began instructing us on how to manage the energy properly. As our lessons progressed, she admitted that she was amazed at the capacity of energy we were able to harness. She had also warned us that another primitivist, once they had learned how to detect the presence of magic, could detect that they were in the presence of someone like themselves. She hadn't said that this detection could also be done by an elf."

Sybal finds the item she is looking for, just as Sapphire finishes her tale.

"Yes, we can detect feral magic, for it is said that our race is derived from it. Now, close your eyes," Sybal says excitedly.

When Sapphire closes her eyes, Sybal pulls Sapphire's hand from her lap, and turns it palm upward.

"Ok, open them," Sybal demands as she drops the object into Sapphire's palm.

Her breath catches in her throat as she stares at the milk-white jewel.

"It is a hoarfrost stone, a symbol of friendship," Sybal explains.

Tears well up in her eyes, and her throat constricts to a point where she is unable to speak. She is totally lost in the significance of the gifts meaning. Since Sybal's return, she seems to be experiencing mixed feelings towards the elf woman. She can't put a finger on exactly what is bothering her most about Sybal, because there are a couple of things she has been noticing in Sybal's actions that are disturbing. Sybal is exceedingly friendly towards her, but distant and almost cold to everyone else. She suspects that Sybal completely dislikes her sister, and resents the deep attachment that she and her sister share. Despite her concerns, she decides to give Sybal the benefit of the doubt.

"Take off that robe, and let me rub this salve on you. You will be eternally grateful, I assure you," Sybal suggests.

She does as she is asked, and lies down upon the blanket after folding her robe into a pillow for her head to rest on. Sybal starts by gently kneading Sapphire's shoulders, and then she begins slowly working her way down Sapphire's entire body. She feels Sapphire tense when she hits sore spots, but by the time she reaches the girls feet, she can tell Sapphire is about to fall asleep.

"If I were a cat, I'd surely be purring," Sapphire murmurs contentedly as she struggles to obey Sybal's command to turn over.

"If you should ever need me, or I you, the hoarfrost stone can be used to guide us to wherever the other is. Utter the words "lilam morbet" and the stone will begin to glow. Once it is invoked, the stone will slowly darken the closer we get to each other, no matter how far we are apart," Sybal explains as she massages some more of the salve into Sapphire's shoulders.

Sybal's hands feel feverishly warm, and are stimulating her in a way that leaves her nearly breathless. The worst of her soreness slowly vanishes as Sybal patiently massages the salve into her hips, thighs, and legs. Sapphire can't stop herself from moaning in pleasure, but the sound is lost when simultaneous shouts of warning ring out from Ruby and Zeke. Her eyes fly open just in time to see Sybal hastily exiting the tent with daggers drawn. Sluggishly rising from the bed, she yanks on her robe, and hastens to follow. By the time she realizes she has forgotten her staff, it is too late to turn back for it.

She becomes instantly mesmerized by what she is seeing. At first she thinks she is still groggy from Sybal's ministrations, because she can't seem to shake off the lethargy she is feeling. Listlessness takes over, and no matter how hard she tries, she can't seem to put her thoughts in order. Very confused, she stands there and wonders what it is she has forgotten. She knows she should be doing something as she stares at the hundreds of tiny creatures flying about the clearing.

She can feel a disruption in the magical energies that she's come to depend on for their stability, and wonders at what this could mean. Briefly, she tries to reach out to touch it with her senses, but the energy resists her attempts to penetrate it. Never has she ever been utterly cut off from it, and she begins to panic. Before fear can overwhelm her, she simply forgets what it is she has been trying to do and stands there with the others entranced by the melodic sounds the creatures begin to make.

Caught up in the melody, we begin to dance and dance, hearing, but unable to heed Sybal's dire warnings to resist. We forgot all about our tiredness, and lose all sense of time. We are still dancing as the sky subtly begins to brighten with the coming of day. As if the pale light is a signal, we collapse in a heap on the ground, and the creatures vanish as if they had never been there at all. They left nothing behind to prove that we hadn't simply imagined them.

Everyone succumbs to a deep slumber where they have fallen

except for Sybal. Though she is exhausted, she is able to resist this part of the magical enchantment, and begins crawling on her hands and knees towards her tent. It takes all of her willpower, but she manages to crawl the distance, and enter her tent. Crawling to her pack, she takes from within it a vial filled with a purplish liquid, and begins fumbling with the stopper. The exhaustion causes her to swoon a moment. In a panic, she fights off the feeling of faintness and frees the stubborn stopper.

Her shaking hands threaten to spill the valuable liquid as she brings the vial to her lips. She regains all her strength and senses after taking a sip of the sweet potion, but because she has taken only a small dose, she knows she must hurry to help the others before the restorative effects of the elixir wear off. Exiting the tent, she starts to head towards Able first, but stops as an idea begins to take shape in her head.

I *could* just leave the others, and carry Sapphire off to safety. That would be an easy way to be rid of the others. All I would have to do is lie to Sapphire to cover up my treachery, and since Sapphire has nowhere else to go, she would probably be willing to come with me. This would give me all the time I would need to determine what has gone awry with my feelings, and also give me time to figure out why the wiccalwa doesn't seem to be affecting Sapphire in any way.

It is possible that the jumbling up of my wiccalwa is due to some form of corruption in the nature of our magic when we are in each other's presence, but only time will be able to unravel this mystery. As suddenly as these thoughts entered her mind, she felt a pain as if she were being stabbed in the heart. Then, it occurs to her as to why.

If it truly is wiccalwa she is experiencing, then she couldn't bring harm to anything that Sapphire deeply cared about. The consequences could be dire. She is a killer, but killing someone in cold blood for her own personal gratification goes against her own personal codes as well as the wiccalwa. She isn't willing to cross over that line and become like Zakinis, a man she now loathes with all her being, and probably wouldn't know wiccalwa if it slapped him in the face. Quickly, and without further hesitation, she begins administering a small dose of the liquid to each of them.

When she revives them with the potion, she quickly explains to Able the need for urgency. He wants to ask questions, but she gives him a look that spurs him into action. They break down the camp in record time, but Sybal can feel her energy sapping quickly before the final tent is taken down. She explains to Able that if they don't wish to carry her, she will have to leave the clearing immediately. Worrying for her safety, Able sends Sapphire with her, and promises Sybal he will not dally. Within minutes of their parting, everyone has made it out of the clearing, and Able uses the trampled grass to guide him to where Sapphire and Sybal have collapsed upon the ground.

CHAPTER FIFTEEN

Takes Two to Tangle

Ruby awoke disoriented, clutching her staff, and laying upon the ground in a sea of tall grass. It appeared to be early afternoon, and memories of the night before were vague. The others still lay where they had collapsed. She knew they had been very lucky, for nobody had been fit to stand guard, and had something come upon them as they slept, they would have surely perished.

Able would have been proud of me for the thought, and for my quick reactions to the situation. None so much as grumbled as I drug them closer to each other, and made them comfortable. I feel a pain of what, jealousy, as I remove Sybal's head from Sapphire's lap? I had always shared everything with Sapphire, and it hurts me that we can't share Sybal's friendship. I believe Sybal can't stand me, and this is beginning to cause a rift between my sister and I. It takes everything I have to drag Zeke over, and I have to rest a moment beside him to catch my breath.

Looking down at his serene face, I straighten his unruly hair with my fingers, unsure why the act causes other feeling to stir within me. We have become friends, and as Sapphire and I drift farther apart, I desperately need a friend. I feel a new pain pierce my heart. Is it again jealousy? Sapphire's and Sybal's friendship is blossoming, while mine remains stagnant, and based only on common interests between Zeke and I. I haven't failed to notice him eyeing Sybal and my sister in the way that men do. Do I only want him to look at me that way, or am I just being selfishly jealous that I can't have what Sapphire has? My hand jerks away when Zeke opens his eyes as my fingertip traces the scar on his face. His eyes seem to bore into me, holding me transfixed, never wavering. It is a searching look that causes my heart to thud in my chest, and my breath to catch in my throat. My eyes are the first to turn away, breaking the captivating spell of his gaze. Heat fills my face as I wonder if he's been able to penetrate my thoughts, surmise my innermost secrets, and come away with what I've been thinking.

I need movement and distance between us to regain my composure, and hide my flaming face. I regain my feet, and keep my back to him as I break the uncomfortable silence.

"Zeke, if you are able to help me, I believe we need to knock down some of this grass so we can see a little better. I don't know how much longer it'll be before the others wake, and we need to make this area better to defend."

I begin trampling the grass, taking my frustrations out on it, but warily keeping an eye out for danger.

"Yes commander," he teases, and begins to help.

When we have cleared a wide circle, I am actually thankful when Sapphire sits up, and removes the strain I feel in having to talk to Zeke alone. Within the hour everyone wakes up, Sybal being the last, and groggiest. She ignores our questions, insisting they can be answered as we travel.

"We have plenty of daylight left, and Able, I strongly urge that we make use of it. The creatures we met meant us no harm, and they don't realize that their enchantment could actually kill us. It's too complicated to explain now, and I will clarify what I mean as we walk. I don't know how far they range, but I know we can't take the risk of staying within their territory."

Able heeds her advice again, and we set off immediately. Though we are still tired, he hurries us along relentlessly, determined to put as much distance as he can between us and the little creatures. We walk at a fast pace, never once stopping to rest, and my legs begin to protest. Able finally allowed us to stop for a few minutes to let us catch our breaths, and eat a quick cold meal. During the short break, Sybal tells us what the creatures were that we had encountered.

"I believe they were a type of sprite or faerie. I have never encountered them before, but the elders have told us many stories about their race. I have even seen three drawings of these fey folk, all were different in their portrayals, and none had resembled what we'd seen last night. It is very rare to encounter them because they are very reclusive. Our teachings have told us of their deadliness though, for their music fills one with temporary strength and energy, and binds one to their will. This is where the danger lies, and one caught in this situation actually becomes a victim of their nature.

When they depart, it leaves one completely drained, and like we experienced, in need of rest that can last as long as their compelling spell. In rare instances, people have escaped to tell of this simply because the fey folk did not return to make merriment with them again. But normally they will return and wait for the victim to awake from the previous experience. They continue to do this until the person no longer wakes. Unwittingly, the fey folk starve the person to death, or cause the victim's body to simply collapse from the exertion."

The end of the story prompts us to depart, and knowing the full extent of the danger, my fear lends new energy to my protesting limbs. That evening finds us departing the endless sea of grass, far from the clearing and its threatening inhabitants. We now look upon rolling hills of forests, pristine, and lush in their greenery. I have lost all track of time, and since the days are growing longer, I presume that spring has given way to summer.

The weather indicates as much because the nights are staying warm, and the days are increasingly getting hotter. Great puffy clouds have been slowly following behind us as we walk, and by the time they catch up to us, their milky whiteness has begun to turn grey. It begins sprinkling on us, and the cool rain is not unwelcome. The drizzle stops at the same moment Able declares that we can stop for the night, and we all laugh at the good timing. The sun returns, and though it has dropped low in the sky, our things dry out quickly in its warmth. As twilight approaches, the setting sun turns the heavens into a mixture of multicolored reds, beautiful and breathtaking.

"We will not have lessons this evening, and from now on, we will have two standing watch during the night. Lessons will resume tomorrow evening, as usual."

We all groan at the news, but accept it without question.

"We will be changing our sleeping arrangements, and I hate to separate you two but I must," he continues, my heart sinking as he looks at Sapphire, and I. "Believe me I have considered your feelings," he hastily adds, cutting off my quick retort, but not before I ask with whom I will be sharing my sleeping quarters with.

"In answer to your question though, you will have a tent to yourself. You will be standing the most important watch of the night with Sybal, and I. The darkest hours are when we are most likely to be attacked, and that is why Sybal and I will stand part of this watch with each of you. Giving you a tent to yourself ensures me you will not be disturbed, Ruby, and that I can be certain that you will be fully rested for your duty. We have taught you how to judge the time by the stars movement, and this new arrangement makes it very important that the person you wake is woke up at the proper time.

Everyone will want their fair share of rest, and you are responsible for judging their waking correctly. Sybal and I will be standing four and a half hours of watch to your three hours, and we'll be cooking the morning and evening meals. Sapphire, you will be sharing Sybal's tent, and your watch begins each evening when we stop to set up camp. Sybal, you will begin your watch halfway through Sapphire's watch. You will wake Ruby halfway through yours, and then me when yours ends.

I will share a tent with Zeke, and wake him for the last watch of the night. I'll spend half that watch with him, and then get some rest before we break camp, unless it's my turn to make the morning meal.

Training in arms will continue, but we will stop earlier in the evening, and complete training before we set up camp."

Able shakes his head at me, refusing to allow me to dispute his decision. He wins the battle of wills and I shift my glare towards Sybal. I nearly bite my tongue in an effort to withhold what I want to say as I watch Sapphire and Sybal exchanging looks and smiles that clearly shows they are pleased with the new arrangements. Grabbing my staff, I stalk off, jealousy eating away at me like a worm in an apple. I take to my bedroll, anger causing sleep to come slowly.

Sybal wakes me from a troubled sleep, and I spend my watch refusing to speak to her or Able for the entire duration. Sleep will not come when I return to my tent, and I lay on my blanket nursing my wounds. I am still awake just before dawn, tired, and restless, so I emerge from my *private* tent to relieve myself. Able has gone to bed when his watch ends, and Zeke nods a greeting to me as I cut through the camp. Along the way, I pass by the tent that Sybal and my sister now share, and peek within when Zeke isn't looking. What my eyes see causes me to completely lose my mind. Sapphire was entwined with Sybal the way we use to always sleep together, and this sparks my rage to the boiling over point.

I return to my tent fully satisfied with myself and lay there anxiously awaiting the result of my misbehavior. It was a childish thing I have done, but I couldn't stop myself at the time. I snuck around their tent and loosened their tent mooring pegs when Zeke's back was turned, hoping that their movements within the tight space would collapse it upon them when they got up. While I am relieving myself, I spot a snake in the underbrush. Its discovery is just fuel for the fire, and in my state of mind, I just can't resist the temptation. I catch it, and slip it within their tent flap, and return to my tent to wait. Their screams are music to my ears, and I barely emerge with my staff in time to see the tent collapse about them.

The tent is in ruins by the time they emerge, and as I watch the commotion, the snake slithers off. I give it my blessing for a long life before it departs, and thank it for a job well done. I have forgotten that Sybal had been bitten by one not long ago, and is probably still petrified from the experience, but somehow I can't feel sorry for my actions. Once Able discovers what has raised the alarm, we stand around laughing about it. I notice Sybal isn't laughing though, and as soon as I can, I quickly return to my tent. I shudder to think what she will do to me if she finds out it is a prank. Surely she can take a joke.

After calming down, Sybal begins to pick up the tent with Sapphire's help. Within minutes she knows the tent has been messed with, and she also guesses by whom, but doesn't mention her suspicions to Sapphire. When Sapphire goes to help Able with the morning meal preparations, she begins investigating the ground for clues. She doesn't want to make accusations before she is sure her suspicions are right. There is no doubt in her mind, as she sorts out all the tracks, that her guesses are correct. She is an expert tracker, and by the time she unravels all the tracks, she has every detail in order, even to the spot where Ruby has picked up the snake. Her first reaction is immediate revenge, but she is afraid that if she confronts Ruby, she will end up doing something she will later regret. Too many things stand in her way for such a rash reaction, and as she begins to calm down, she begins to smile.

It begins drizzling again when we set off that morning, but becomes a heavier rain as the day progresses. Though we are soon soaked through and through, our footing is good, and we continue to make good time.

"A red sky in the eve is but a sailor's reprieve, for tis rain it will spawn, by the grey light of dawn" Able comments as we hunch over our cold meal that afternoon.

The break is short, and the meal is eaten in silence. As we rise to set out once again, we reluctantly remove our hoods, not willing to suffer another of Able's tirades. It is another of his rules that we don't like, but makes perfect sense. One's vision is limited by a hood, and even more so by the rain. It is a miserable way to travel, and by evening, everyone is short tempered. But our moods improve when the rain stops, and the sun comes out to greet us.

After practice, we set up camp in the crest of a flat hilltop, which affords us a spectacular view of a rainbow that is now arching across the sky. The beauty of the surrounding area in the twilight is remarkable, and the presence of the rainbow heightens it dramatically. This high up, the brush is very sparse, and it makes guarding it that much easier. It also makes it harder for Able to slip away to see if he can follow the rainbow to its end. He pretends the idea has never crossed his mind, and though we tease him mercilessly, he continues to talk incessantly about the subject.

"Hogwash and fiddlesticks, Able," Sybal spouts when she overhears Able speaking to Zeke of the gold one could find there, "Tis only twaddle; a story for children and crazy men like you to believe, it tis. Next, you'll be telling them they'll find leprechauns dancing on them piles of gold."

Sheepishly cowed by her remarks, Able drops the subject. Before it is even dark, tiredness overcomes me, and I go to my tent. I lay on my blanket for a while thinking, and then giggling as I recall the prank of this morning. It isn't long before I begin to doze off, scratching at my legs from the bed bugs that are becoming more persistent as the days get warmer. It seems the more I scratch the fiercer their biting becomes, and it is becoming exasperating. Suddenly I am fully awake, frantically scraping the bugs off of me. It feels like a hundred angry bees are stinging my legs and the more I move, the more they bite me. I try to dive out of the tent flap, but my feet tangle up in my blanket, causing me to crash into the side of the tent. My screams can be heard all the way to Canaan, and as my tent collapses about me, it dawns on me that I have been found out.

CHAPTER SIXTEEN
Animal Magnetism

I've had six different names, and I've been five different animals since being afflicted by what I've come to assume is a curse, or a backfired spell. I don't remember having made anyone that mad at me to have had them hurl a curse my way, and I can't remember casting a spell that had gone awry, but nevertheless, this is now the immortal life I lead. I've been the familiar rat, bat, two different kinds of fowl, and a cow. The last being the most challenging and awkward for a man turned animal who is now compelled to attach himself as a companion to another mortal who possesses the use of magic. I'd just gotten use to being a cow when my life was abruptly cut short by hungry peasants who dared poach me from the warlock I'd become a familiar to. He hadn't been a good master anyway, so there was no love lost there. Instead of my companionship, he was always forgetting about me in the field for months at a time, while he studied his tomes of wizardry. Immortality does have its drawbacks when one is forced to endure it in this way.

It is just one of the many drawbacks to being an immortal. I am subjected to endure the torture of retaining human instincts while being thrust into another beings body that is incapable of accomplishing many of the tasks I would like to perform with it. The potency of this spell never ceases to impress me, and as I discover more of its subtle persecutions, my hatred for spells of this nature increases. The spell is designed to make me want to welcome death, but because it deprives me of this simple pleasure, I can only hope for something to happen that will reverse the effects of it, and at last allow me make the journey into the netherworld.

MORTAL CONQUESTS OF THE DARK AGES

True to the nature of my affliction, fate once again brings a new master my way, and I am compelled to forsake my easy life to become a familiar with the fiery red headed woman below. Alarmed, I wonder why she's screaming at the top of her lungs loud enough to wake the dead. I chatter amusedly as I watch, but nearly fall off the tree limb I'm on, when I feel her pain. This is another abuse both my master and I suffer at the hands of this powerful enchantment. Once the compulsion takes full effect, there is a linking of our life's energy, and if either of us are wounded or just suffer anything painful at all, the other suffers the same thing too. This linking has resulted in the death of me in the past; because the creatures I possess have a lot less life energy than that of my new masters.

Whatever is biting her is making me itch like crazy, and the stinging pain from the attack is nearly unbearable. I scramble to the ground real fast, not wanting to fall from the limb I'm on as I try to scratch. This is not a fine way to start our new relationship, but at least I'm still alive. There are many ways to die, but now my chances of suffering death have doubled, and two of my deaths have happened at the ignorant hands of my masters. My rat form was killed outright when my first master cast a spell that backfired. When I was a bat, I was bludgeoned to death by the staff of another master with whom I didn't even get a chance to become a familiar with; that was a learning experience, and one mistake I am not apt to allow again. If I'd known the mage was terrified of bats, I wouldn't have approached him as suddenly as I had. To say the least, I've learned to come near my new masters with a bit more caution.

Unsure of what is going on, but extremely curious, I edge up for a closer look at their camp. I'm definitely not willing to approach this woman at this time. She appears to be extremely upset, and from the glare in her eyes, she shows the disposition of one who is ready to commit murder. Instead, my goal is to learn more about why she is here in the first place, and gauge the disposition of her traveling companions.

I am hoping her demeanor isn't evil, for I've learned that a master so inclined to have a temperament of this nature is quite against my human nature, and the nature of the creatures I've inhabited so far.

I learn nothing as I creep about in the darkness, and the guards standing watch aren't talking, though I do hear them chuckling to themselves in the dark. I do learn my new master's name is Ruby by the time she's finished restoring her tent, and I presume my Ruby has disappeared within it for the night. By my third jaw cracking yawn, I decide that tomorrow's another day, and I'm about to leave when one of the guards removes her hood within a few feet of where I'm hiding.

Stunned, I have to look three times to make sure my eyes are not deceiving me in the darkness, and three times my eyes confirm that my new master is standing right there in front of me. Now how in the nine Hells had she done that? Confused, I try to detect magic using the limited capacity I still retain from once being a powerful magician myself, but I do not detect anything. My magic capabilities are limited due to the intelligence of the creature whose body I reside in. Unfortunately, this also limits their potency, and though this can be aggravating, I am not one to look a gift horse in the mouth. I am completely baffled and out of sorts with what I am seeing, and decide the answer to the puzzling situation will present itself in due time. Tired from a day of feasting and play, I decide to worry over this dilemma tomorrow in favor of a good night's sleep in my drey.

The morning is usually my favorite time of day in this form. I find a squirrel's life is not too bad, for we are quite adventurous creatures when not gathering food for the long cold months of winter. Today, I am a bit melancholy as I approach the camp. I always get this way when I am forced to leave what has become a normal way of life to the creature whose body I have possessed since birth. Just the thought of leaving my drey and hoard is distressing me, for I also have to share this creatures feeling and fears when it comes time to attach myself to a new master. But my will is stronger than the creatures, and it's acknowledged, regardless of the creature's reluctance to leave when the time comes. I worry at a pine seed taken from a cleft in the tree where my drey is, and watch them disassemble their camp. I'm going to miss my drey, for it has taken many hours of hard work to design the nest to my liking. Pushing those thoughts away, I listen as the others good naturedly tease my new master in regards to her experiences the night before, and I'm able to tell from heated looks between her, and the half-elf they call Sybal, that no love is lost between them.

I discover the reason behind the chance encounter last night with who I had believed was my new master. It turns out that my master is a twin. I've never seen two women so identical in appearance before, but I knew that it was possible. Having this minor detail cleared up is a major relief, but I am still frustrated because I haven't yet had an opportunity to approach my new master in a way that will not get me killed. They set off to the northeast, and I tag along trying to keep out of site by using whatever cover I can find.

I am familiar with the terrain we are passing through until we reach the end of what I call my territory, and as we cross my territorial boundaries, homesickness does nothing to ease my depressed state. They stop once for a quick meal, and I take the opportunity to approach my Ruby because I am growing afraid. I might be able to bully the instincts of the squirrel into doing what I want most of the time, but sometimes they are strong enough to override me. In this case, wandering around in unfamiliar terrain is not a healthy thing to do when one is near the top of the food list of most meat eating predators. In light of this, it becomes imperative for me to force the meeting with my Ruby, and come out of hiding.

"Look, isn't it beautiful," Ruby says as I scurry into view while she is looking my way.

That is a good sign, and I slink closer to her as the others turn to look me over. I peer intently into her eyes, compelling her to feel the bond we now share, and urging her acceptance of me by casting a charm spell to heighten the effect. It works. It always works, even without the addition of the charm spell, for she cannot long refuse the allure of this controlling curse. After last night's fright, and the storm that followed, I do not want to scare her in front of the others, and subject myself to an untimely death due to insensitive planning, nor do I wish to become their evening meal.

"You seem to attract unusual creatures," the one called Zeke claims after several moments pass.

I have used those moments before he spoke, to close the distance between Ruby and I. She ignores the laughter the remark triggers, and I can sense her apprehension when I stop within arm's reach of where she is sitting. I cower before her until her fear subsides, and she becomes the bolder. My non-aggressiveness has reassured her that I mean her no harm, and as her fingers reach tentatively out to touch my soft fur, I close my eyes. Her touch is light, and calms the rapid beating of my squirrel heart. This approaching of a human goes against the entire nature of this creature I'm in, and it takes a battle of wills to quell its anxiety. When I am sure she is enthralled, I crawl forward on my belly like a dog seeking forgiveness, and rest my head on her foot. Nobody breaks the silence as our bonding takes place, and I can tell that they are in awe of this unusual occurrence.

"Will you look at that," Zeke says, and that's when I feel the probe of magic.

"Ruby, I sense magic is at work here, and it's very powerful magic indeed. I suggest caution," Sybal says, "or, have you summoned this creature to be your companion?"

By the look on her face it's obvious Ruby doesn't know what she is talking about, and I don't miss seeing that she is deeply disturbed by the question. She shoots her sister a withering look, and Sapphire mouths the words, "she knows", when she thinks nobody is looking. I'm completely at a loss as to what this exchange means, and bewildered, I hope for the best. Thankfully my new master is quick to rebound from whatever just transpired, and I'm fully cheering her on as she scornfully rebukes the half-elf for saying such a stupid thing.

"What's the matter Sybal, are you envious because it picked me to befriend? At least this squirrel has some sense when it comes to choosing with whom it wishes to make an acquaintance with."

I open my eyes in time to see that her last remark is intended for her sister's benefit, and the quick exchange of angry looks between them, makes me now fully understand what is happening between the three women. Unheeding the half-elves warning, Ruby cautiously eases her hand under me, and I allow her to pick me up and set me protectively in her lap.

"I warn you Ruby, I sense magic at work here, and there is no telling if this magic is good or bad. Able, I clearly beseech thee to intervene here."

"I believe I will intervene. I think it is high time you two call an end to this rivalry. It's not helping me, and it's beginning to affect everyone's mood. I have enough problems to deal with, and your petty differences are not among them. All I see is a squirrel that may be hungry, and since Ruby is eating nuts and berries, maybe it came to her asking for a handout. See? Look at the poor thing eat as if it hasn't had a meal in days. I clearly think that the creature is harmless."

Having spoken his peace, their leader stalks off mumbling something about women that I don't quite catch. My silent blessings follow behind him, for I am quite pleased with his judgment. When he mentions that I might be hungry, Ruby offers me a palm full of nuts and berries. I begin devouring the food like I'll never get another meal to convince everyone that Able is correct in his assessment of me. This does the trick, and swings more favor my way.

Sybal is fit to be tied that things aren't going her way, and I know I have an enemy in her when she hisses, "Suit yourself, it does look like it could use a little meat on its bones, skinny squirrels don't make good soup."

I don't like her tone of voice, nor the critical way she is looking at me, and neither do the others. It is clear to see that everyone is on Ruby's side, and this unity causes Sybal to angrily walk off. Despite his plea, it is clear that their leader's rebuke has fallen on deaf ears, and has perhaps stiffened their resolve to do anything but give in to his request. I say this because prior to my master setting me aside when it is time to resume their journey, the unladylike gestures the half-elf and my unforgiving master exchange, read volumes into what they think about Able's suggestion. Sapphire seems to be the most distressed, and must feel caught between a rock and a hard place where the two women are concerned. It is clear that she finds it difficult to take sides in the matter because of her friendship with one, and the love she has for the other. It is probably a healthy idea for me to stay as far away from Sybal as possible, and let her get over it. Following my own advice, I spend the rest of the afternoon scampering along behind Ruby's heels.

CHAPTER SEVENTEEN

Courting Disaster

The endless expanse of rolling hills and dense yew forests we travel through become monotonous, and after a while we become bored. But boredom leads to carelessness. Sybal stops us on a hilltop long enough to survey the terrain. Why, I have no idea. You've seen one hill; you may as well say you've seen them all. Uninterested, I look at the blue sky. It's the bluest I've ever seen a sky, weird, and completely cloudless. Having to run beside me as I walk, Able's lesson for this day is boring me. I've lost interest in his annoying chatter nearly a half hour ago, and he knows it.

"Look at how high those hills are in the distance. Able, should we take the northeast, or northwest fork of this road?" Sybal asks, drawing my eyes to look past the twins.

They haven't said a word to each other since the scrawny squirrel incident took place, but as soon as Hell freezes over, I'm sure they'll be chatting away like two squirrels in a drey. Able gives up trying to get me to pay attention to his lesson, and runs up to join Sybal. He studies the far horizon a few minutes before commenting, and I can see he isn't happy.

"I don't know Sybal, my map doesn't have half these roads on it. At this pace we may never get to Wynelvenest. Have ye any idea as to where we're at?" Able asks apprehensively.

Sybal looks around, but we can see she's unsure of where we are.

"I have no idea," she admits, causing me to ask the most stupid of questions.

"Are we getting close to this great wall you told us about?"

Like I said, it was a stupid question. Able had claimed this wall had been built from one side of the island to the other, and you probably couldn't miss seeing it, not to mention that we've only been traveling for a couple of weeks now, so we are probably a little ways from it still. I see the others looking at me funny, and I shrug. This is what happens when one falls into a dreary routine. Constant inaction dulls the brain. Able simply rolls his eyes at me.

"Zeke, I think you will know the answer to that when we do. But, since you mention it, I will tell you a little more about the wall. It's rumored that the soldiers have stopped guarding certain areas of the wall, and now people have begun tearing it down to use the block to build homes. Even if this is true, I'm sure we'll see some kind of rubble, or something to indicate we've crossed it. It won't be much longer before we see Hadrian's Wall; at least I hope it doesn't take too much longer than I have planned. Our goal is to reach Lakenhall by fall, and we should have plenty of time to make that deadline as long as nothing happe…" Able's words are cut off by an ear splitting shriek.

The cry is immediately taken up by other voices that seem to come from all around us. Our surprise is complete, and our reactions are slowed because of it. The hideous creatures take advantage of our slow response, and are upon us before we can even form the protective ring that we'd been practicing.

"Hell's fire and brimstone, what the hell are they?" I holler out as I struggle to draw my sword.

One of the creatures is charging at me at an alarming, ground covering run. The curved sword it's brandishing at me makes my knees go weak from fear, and I have a sinking feeling that goes clear to the pit of my stomach. These are no wild barbarians, but very tall battle hardened veterans who look to have survived many a bloody skirmish. The half-plate suits of armor they're wearing and the large oval shields they carry indicate this very clearly. Even their shields are designed to maim or kill their opponents, for from the center of them protrudes a deadly spike.

I suddenly feel a bit underdressed for the occasion, and since I've had no experience fighting someone so readily equipped, it's a wonder I've not pissed my trousers. This is also the point where I realize the creature isn't giving me a warm hearty greeting, and that if this damn sword doesn't clear leather before he reaches me, my time might have been better spent just kissing my arse goodbye. My first thought is that they are half-orc's, because they closely resemble that brute we killed in the alley. The way my luck's been, we probably killed someone important back there, and these brutes were sent out after us to get revenge. One can't help thinking like this when ones arse is puckered to the point that my backside resembles a frog standing up in tights.

"Bloody hell, they're hobgoblins!" I hear Sybal scream as she engages in battle with two of them.

It is hard to explain how I feel when my sword finally comes free. Elation of course, but that is not what I mean. My heart is beating at a frantic pace, and I begin to experience the other things that I had not experienced in my first real fight. I dive to the side to avoid being run over by the charging hobgoblin, and the quickness of the sidestep sends it right on past me. My eyes seem to be taking in the entire scene at once, but also they seem to have narrowed in on the creature that just sped past me. Able told me that this is called battle vision, or an awareness of everything that is happening around you.

I would have hoped my first experience with this kind of vision would have allowed me to see that we were faring well, but as the narrower focus of this vision watches the creature who just went charging past me, I am convinced that it is not going well at all. Though I put every effort into trying to pursue the brute before he slams his spike pointed shield into Sapphire's unprotected back, I'm unable to catch him. He drives the spike deep, and bowls her over like a large boulder rolling down a steep hill. Sapphire's agonizing cry puts new life in my feet, but I ignore her. The hobgoblin is now intent on bashing his shield into Ruby, and I hurl myself at him like a madman to prevent it. Despite the agony she must be suffering, Sapphire lunges at him from the ground, and trips him up by grabbing at his ankles before he reaches her sister.

I scream out no, but the sounds of battle drowns out my warning, and Ruby turns her attention away from the hobgoblin she's embattled with when she hears her sister distressing howl of pain. The hobgoblin on the ground is trying to get up, so I drive my sword into his spine, but it doesn't go in. Instead my hand goes numb clear up to my elbow, and Sir Hobgoblin rolls to the side, turns, and tries to separate my legs from my torso. I leap high in the air, and slightly forward, intending to plant both feet in the hobgoblin's chest. His sword misses me, and hits the pack Ruby had dropped to the ground by her feet when we stopped to talk. The pack hits Ruby behind the legs, and causes her to stagger, thus saving her from being cleaved head to crotch by a downward swing of the hobgoblin's sword while her head was turned. My feet land squarely in the center of the downed hobgoblin's breastplate, and I drive my sword into his eye, since it's the only opening in the helm that I see. My wider vision sees several other things happening at once.

Sapphire's eyes are closed, and she isn't moving. Sybal is in big trouble. There are now three hobgoblins driving her down the slope of the hill, and she is trying to fight them off with only her daggers. There's a hobgoblin on the ground at Able's feet, and as my sword ends the life of the hobgoblin beneath me, he rushes off to help Sybal. I can't describe what I felt as I helplessly watched that blade descend down on Ruby a moment before. Something triggered a dread in my heart that was more wounding than any injury I'd ever sustained in my life. In that one brief moment, I realized how much she meant to me. Invigorated by this feeling, I hurl myself at the hobgoblin attacking her, but again I'm too late.

Before I can reach her side, I'm momentarily blinded when the hobgoblin's sword strikes Ruby's staff. In that instance, the area around us became dark, and surreal. Tendrils of silvery white light danced down the hobgoblin's curved blade before arching out to encompass his entire body in a halo of shimmering light. The hobgoblin begins to convulse violently, and I can smell the searing of his flesh. The intensity of energy these rays produce make the hair stand up on my head, and I stay my sword arm in fear the energy would harm me if I strike at the creature. It lasts only a heartbeat, yet time seems to have come to a complete stop. Then suddenly the hobgoblin is thrown a few feet backwards, and lands hard on its back. The hobgoblin is lying on the ground unmoving, and I can smell the rancid odor of burnt flesh. I see relief in Ruby's eyes, and in mine I know she is seeing disbelief, and horror as we glance at each other. It is a normal reaction to what I've just seen, but I believe she mistakes my reaction for something akin to disgust, and in that same moment, I know I've hurt her feelings deeply. The blood drains from her face when she looks past me towards her motionless sister.

"Go to her, I'll help the others," is all I can say as I dash off to help Sybal and Able.

The fighting is well down the hill, and I cannot yet see how Sybal and Able are faring. The hobgoblins battle cry has changed, and by the sound of it, I can tell that they feel victory is at hand. My pounding feet finally bring me to where I can see the struggle going on below the crest of the hill. Able's sword is like a snakes flickering tongue, and though he appears to be unhurt, I can tell he is tiring under their relentless attack. Sybal is down on one knee, desperately trying to fend off the blows of two attackers. The higher ground gives the hobgoblins the advantage, and will be to my advantage as well when I join the fray. I remain silent as I approach, hoping to gain surprise, and at least kill one of the two on Sybal before they realize I am upon them.

Silently, I swing at a spot where a hobgoblin's helm and cuirass meet. The two separate slightly, and my sword bites deep into the tender flesh of his neck. Pulsing geysers of red liquid begin to spurt out, splattering my hands and face. My arms throb from the impact, and I lose my grip on the sword because my fingers have gone numb. The sound of the contact is like that which resounds when a hammer strikes an anvil. The suddenness of my attack distracts the other hobgoblin bashing at Sybal, and in the brief second he glances to assess the danger, Sybal uses it to her advantage by thrusting both daggers up into the hobgoblin's throat. The fight goes out of the last hobgoblin, but not before he succeeds in knocking Able down with his shield. I wretch my sword loose from the dead hobgoblin at my feet, and start to pursue him, but Able calls me back.

"Let him go, Zeke. There may be others hiding in the tree line."

His words stop me cold in my tracks, and when I turn back, I break into a run. Able is kneeling on the ground, leaning on his sword, and gasping for breath. But that is not why I am running. I run because Sybal is slumped over the body of the hobgoblin she's killed, and she isn't moving at all.

"Sybal," I groan, gently shaking her to illicit a response.

"I'm fine, Zeke, but I've been wounded. Help me up."

I help Sybal to her feet just as the fleeing hobgoblin disappears into the trees. She staggers, sways, and I have to catch her in my arms before she falls. I pick her up, amazed at how light she is, and begin carrying her up the slope with Able leading the way.

"Zeke, we must go back and get their armor, and weapons. If we don't, they will," Able states.

Sybal is bleeding from numerous places, and her fine garments are in tatters. Her eyes are closed, and her breathing is ragged.

"Able, Sapphire is hurt real bad, and Sybal isn't looking too good either. They need immediate attention. Do you really think we should go back to get those things right now, and leave them with only Ruby to guard them?"

Able shoots me a withering look.

"I'm not that greedy, and insensitive," he exclaims with a hurt look upon his face.

"Able, I didn't mean it that way! I'm just worried about getting attacked again, and... Oh, never mind."

My anger and tone of voice makes him turn around again.

"Forget it, I believe you. Look, all I want to do is prevent that armor, and those weapons from getting back into their hands. That's all. Do you think you can get it without me? If so, I'll stay with them, and attend the wounded with Ruby."

Pacified, I grin to let him know I hold no hard feelings, and the subject is forgotten. When we get back to where the others are, we find that Sapphire is miraculously unhurt, but in a foul mood.

"Look at this," she wails holding up her pack to show us that there is a gaping hole in it.

"Just thank the Gods that it went into the pack, and not in your back," Able declares gruffly, dropping down beside Sybal as I lay her on the ground. "I would think we have other concerns than your pack right now, so get on that slope and watch the tree line for Zeke as he recovers those weapons and armor below. Ruby, put that damn animal down, and get over there and watch our rear."

Able's no nonsense tone sends the girls scurrying, and I flee down the hill to avoid drawing his ire my way. It takes three trips to strip the three hobgoblins, and I am sore tired when I crest the hill bearing the last of the armor. Able is tying the cloth ends together on the last bandage he is working on, and Sybal is now sitting up complaining that she is fine.

"Scratches can become tainted, and some of those deeper wounds will need a poultice spread on them to speed the healing. I'll make it later when we find a safer place to stop. Do you think you can walk long enough for me to find us a place that is easier to defend?"

Sybal nods her head, and stands up. Her first steps are unsteady, but she continues to walk around insisting she just needs to work the stiffness from her muscles. She is doing better by the time Able finishes making a litter to drag our newly acquired gear, and she even stands a short watch while Ruby eats her noon meal. Able's ire hadn't dissipated, and he lets us have it for letting our guard down, though he claims it is totally his fault for allowing us to do it in the first place.

"Let this be a lesson well learned, and be thankful no one was killed, or captured," Able emphasizes heatedly.

I quietly mention what I saw happen to the hobgoblin that Ruby had struck with her staff, and by the time Able is done questioning Ruby, we all know now that Sapphire and Ruby are both capable of casting magical spells. Ruby also confesses that the staff she is carrying had been her mother's magical staff, and that she isn't sure what it may be fully capable of doing.

"We have to travel in the same direction that the hobgoblin ran off in. I don't think I need to say more. But I do want to say this. My people seek Canaan for many reasons, but the most important of these reasons is to shake off the bonds of persecution, and create a society of people who are equal no matter what race they are, or what abilities they possess." As he speaks, Able eyes the twins, and gives Sybal a meaningful look when he mentions race.

I can see his words have impressed all three of them.

"There is one last thing. Ruby, you will always watch our left flank when we travel. Sapphire, you will watch overhead. Zeke, you will watch our right flank. Sybal and I will watch the rear, and front. This will be done even when we stop for our noon meal, or for any other reason. Do I make myself clear?"

Nods of affirmation come from all around, and Able gives the order to resume our journey. The sun has just past its zenith as we descend the slope, and cautiously approach the unfriendly tree line.

CHAPTER EIGHTEEN
North Hill

Hobgoblins are stalking our back trail, and there are only a few hours of daylight left. Everyone's on edge.

"Shouldn't we just leave it?" I ask worriedly.

We are deep within the forest, and seriously encumbered by the litter that insists on snagging every root along our path. We begin walking down a very steep hill, and after the litter has turned over twice, I am becoming more than frustrated.

"Zeke, your right in your thinking, and I know it's slowing us down, but it's more important than ever that we don't let these things get back into their hands," Able replies, looking nervously over his shoulder.

Sybal looks like she is about to drop from exhaustion. She keeps putting one foot in front of the other, and despite her weariness, she manages to keep up.

"Look!" Sapphire shouts, pointing through the tree line.

"Now how in the nine Hells did we not see that?" Able exclaims, appearing to be very overjoyed to see the cluster of buildings in the valley below, for we dearly need supplies, rest, and refuge from the enemy pursuing us.

"We will not be passing this town up. We will go into it for supplies, and a much needed rest."

A chorus of excited cheers erupts at Able's words, and I try to do a jig, but my dancing more closely resembles a man whose pants are full of fire ants than anything else. It's embarrassing.

"Quiet, and listen." Able commands; something he is getting very good at here lately. "As of now, you two are married, and Sapphire, you're with them because you're all going to a relative's wedding in Mamucium. We'll have to disguise Sybal somehow, and me too, since I may not be welcome here either.

Sybal can pass as a sick daughter and I as your very shy son. They probably haven't seen many twins, so that should create enough gossip to keep them from paying too close attention to us children. With the hobgoblins right behind us, our warning will create a big disturbance in the town, and most folks will be too worried about their own affairs to pay much attention to ours."

Since I am to play Ruby's husband, an act that makes us both turn red in the face, I decide to have a little fun. I ask Ruby for a practice kiss, just so I can warm up to the role of playing her husband.

"Perhaps, if you think you must. But since you feel the need to jest at the sake of my maidenly honor, I think not, for I'd rather kiss a horse's rear than give you the satisfaction of treating me like a common tavern wench."

Her reply is startling not only to me, but especially to Sapphire and the others. I stand there speechless as Ruby trounces away. Able looks like he is about to pee in his trousers, and the mouths of the others are open so wide, you'd have thought they were going to bob for apples in a barrel. Women!

Able begins going over the story he wants us to tell as we prepare to enter the town.

"First, go to a town guard or the beadle, and tell your tale. Say we've been running away from some creatures that are trying to attack us, and have become horribly lost. Claim that we are going to Mamucium for a wedding. I believe Mamucium should be somewhere near here if I have correctly calculated the distance we have traveled. You can say Sybal is a fragile child that may not live out the year due to her illnesses. If anyone offers to look at her, just say everything has been done for her, and you're only wish is that she not be disturbed, or say anything that will keep them away from us.

As soon as you can, ask the official where we can find lodging, and try to appear dogged tired so he'll get the hint that we need rest."

Able pulls on his cloak, and pulls his hood up to hide his face. Sybal lies down on the litter and we cover her with blankets. We also use blankets to hide all the hobgoblins gear, and our own weapons as well. Able tells Ruby to leave the squirrel here in the woods, but though she agrees, I see her hide the animal in her pack when he isn't looking. I didn't mention seeing her do this to anyone, for I would rather chase Hell with a bucket of cold water than incur her wrath again.

"Do you have any questions?" Able asks.

We shake our heads no, and Able motions for Ruby and I to start dragging the litter down the hill. Able follows at the foot of the litter, and keeps an eye out for danger as we descend into the valley below.

We are arriving a little off the beaten path, and have to cut across some fields where a few boys are tending a flock of sheep.

"Perfect. Go straight to them, and warn them about the hobgoblins. I'm sure one of them will run ahead to the town with a warning." Able instructs softly.

We head towards them, and try to draw their attention. To dramatize the occasion, and make our distress more realistic, I begin to wave my arms at them like a madman. Ruby catches on to the act, and leans into me like she is dogged tired, and needs my support. Her closeness triggers one of those unwanted reactions that men my age go through when a pretty woman does the unexpected, as in touching you like they know you. As one of the herders approaches, my only hope is that my growing concern isn't too noticeable.

The news we carry sends the master herder running across the field to give the warning to the town. Other workers come up to us to ask questions, and do their best to answer ours. We learn that we are in North Hill, and that there have been numerous sightings and attacks in the area all spring. None of the workers even know where Mamucium is, so we ask where we can find shelter. We learn that there isn't an abbey, or monastery, in the area, but there is a man and his wife who board travelers in their barn. The bell of the town crier begins sounding the alarm as we draw closer to the town, and as Able has predicted, the people are quickly reacting. We see several boys run across the fields to carry the warning to the outlaying farms, and the townspeople begin gathering their children, animals, and other valuable possessions into their homes. Hay makers, herders, and men plowing the fallow fields, begin bringing in animals and equipment when the town reeve orders them to do so. We enter the town, and are immediately surrounded by town officials. The town steward, having more authority than either the beadle or reeve, questions us thoroughly. His concern for our welfare keeps the questioning short, and we are given an escort to the home of Henry, and his wife Gabriela.

The couple's home is a standard wood frame home, plastered with wattle and daub, and roofed with thatch. It has a front and side door, and one tiny window. Since wood is too expensive, the doorways are covered with curtains to keep out the blowing street dust. People in towns like this are indebted to the king, or his son the duke. The towns are controlled by hireling of the nobles to insure they aren't being cheated at tax time. The people pay heavy taxes for the privilege of using the land, and are not allowed to cut down trees, fish, or even hunt without the ruling noble's permission, because all the lands resources belong to them alone. Their chances of owning the land they work are slim, even after several generations of toil. Most are so indebted that their lives are just a mere step away from becoming slaves to the nobles. The nobles keep a tight fist on the prosperity of the people, and after taxes, most barely have enough left to survive the winter. Those who can pay the heavy taxes usually don't have enough left over to afford the steep price of the land they live on, and it is all they can do to keep their heads above water.

Henry and Gabriela's home depicts that they are managing to keep their heads above water. The house is only a one room affair, and quite small, but it is well maintained. Another sign of their prosperity is the large barn behind their home, for this is a luxury that most folks can't afford. Our escort is the town's pinder, a man who is responsible for gathering in stray animals, and putting them in the pinfold. He is not one for conversation, but he does take the time to introduce us to the couple, and tells of our encounter with the hobgoblins. Then he begs leave of us, and hurries off to help the reeve.

"You poor things," Gabriela clucks, separating me from the others as she escorts the twins and my *children* to the barn.

Henry is a jovial, thickset man, who is short of sight, and has a way at peering at you as if he can't see you clearly. He also seems nervous when we begin to dicker over the price of our stay. Able has already given me some silver coins, and I hope that they will be enough.

"I'll only take gold, silver, or copper coins, but since everyone's begun to hoard coins, I'm willing to work out some other arrangements," Henry admits sheepishly.

It is getting to where nobody will take the brass coins of the Romans anymore, and since coins are getting scarce, bartering is the usual way of obtaining what one wants.

"I have silver coins," I say shaking my coin pouch for emphasis.

His eyes light up at the sound, and he moistens his lips repeatedly as he tries to think of a fair price.

"Well now, we offer simple pottage and dark bread for the noon, and evening meals, and Gabriela makes a tasty flat pan cake in the morn. Each meal is served with a tankard of ale, or fresh cow's milk. If ye be one who likes his spirits, ye can go to the tavern across the street and drink your fill. I'll settle for three silver coins to room and board the lot of you tonight, and if you're planning to stay longer, I think four silver coins a day would be quite fair. We don't offer a bath, but you can take one in the river if ye be so inclined."

The price is a fair one, but I still try to haggle it down a bit anyway, and am unsuccessful for my efforts. I pay him for the night, since

I don't know how long Able intends for us to stay and stand there looking down the main street. Henry fidgets, obviously eager to swap gossip, but is hesitant to ask any questions. These days, one doesn't ask pointed questions of strangers, but waits for them to bring up whatever they wish to talk about.

I watch a man put his cow, a pig, and an ox into his house, a common practice when one doesn't have a barn, and since the loss of the precious animals could mean life or death, they are more than willing to share their home in this manner with the beasts.

"Henry, why is all that wood piled up in the center of the street?" I ask, breaking the uncomfortable silence.

"Why tis for Liþa, otherwise known as the Sonnwend, or Midsummer Solstice to some, and though it's considered a pagan festival, its one we still observe here in North Hill. We build a huge fire for tomorrow night's festivities. It's great fun. Young men and women leap over the flames to see who can jump the highest, because it's thought that the crops will grow to the height of the highest jumper. This may just be an old wife's tale, but it tends to pick up everyone's spirits."

Sybal has taught us some of the more popular pagan festivals of the land, and though they are frowned upon by the Roman Church, many of the festivals still flourish in towns without the church's influence. The festival means we are at the end of se Ærra Liþa, or June. After asking what day it is, Henry tells me it is Sæterndæg, or Saturday. The townsmen are beginning to gather in a large group to hunt down the hobgoblins, and I notice most are only carrying farming tools as a weapon. Gabriela returns, and enters the house after reassuring me that everyone is resting comfortably. Henry begs my leave when he sees the men gathering to hunt down the hobgoblins, and disappears into his house. He comes back out bearing a badly rusted sword. He is also trying to shake off a very upset wife, who is following on his heels, and lecturing him every step of the way.

"Henry, put that sword up. You aren't in any condition to go traipsing about in the woods fighting monsters. Let those younger men take care of this," she begs, but it is obvious Henry had no intensions of doing any such thing. Henry winks at me, and then gives his tearful wife a peck on the cheek.

"Now, don't ye fret woman. I've survived three wars, and numerous encounters with foul beasts, and I won't stand around and let someone else defend my hearth. These folks are probably starved, and your time might be better spent preparing the pottage, than worrying about me."

Gabriela, knowing that it is hopeless to argue, flees into the house sobbing.

I offer to join the hunt, but Henry insists we've been through enough today. I can tell he's pleased that I've offered, and that in doing so, I've gained his respect.

"You stay here and rest. We've enough capable men to handle this problem. I'd appreciate you keeping an eye on my missus, and should something happen whilst were away, I'd be beholden to ye for any help you'd give her."

When he joins the growing group of hunters, I watch him inspire courage amongst the boys in the group that appear to be a little afraid. When one would show signs of wavering, he'd make his way over to him, and take a moment to bolster his spirits. He is not the leader of the group, but I have no doubt that this man has led others before. They depart in a ragtag formation, nearly a hundred strong, and someone begins to sing. The singer is soon joined by others, and as they march away, their measured footfalls keep time with the song's rhythm.

Shouts from loved ones assail them from all directions as they march down the street. Caught up in the spirit, I walk with the crowd to the edge of town, shouting with the others my wishes for their safe and speedy return. When they have disappeared into the trees, I return to the town with those who are left behind. The town only has one long street, so I familiarize myself with its layout as I walk. I try to stay out of the way of those around me who are still busy securing anything of value, but this is becoming harder to do as the street fills with livestock. They seem to expect that a raid is imminent, and even the women are carrying sickles, and other farming tools for protection. I stop a few people to ask where certain shops are located, and though the people I ask are busy, they are friendly enough to take the time to tell me where I can find them.

Every merchant has closed up early because of the situation, and since I can't get a look at their wares, I decide to check on how the others are faring in the barn.

CHAPTER NINETEEN
Emotional Entanglements

Our space in the barn is better than expected. A curtain lends privacy to several large stalls that have been converted into sleeping quarters, and each stall has a box filled with straw to sleep in. There is a stool to sit on, and pegs have been hammered into the wall for hanging one's garments. Each stall boasts its own chamber pot, wash basin, and water pitcher.

For light, a large lantern hangs from a center beam in the middle of the building. Able is quick to inform me that Gabriela has asked that we not use candles or any other illumination in the barn during our stay. Fire is always a danger in a barn, and I can understand her concerns, having grown up on a farm myself. Able is inconspicuously keeping watch while the others are asleep. I am bone achingly tired, but out of habit, I take the time to finish some chores that need doing in Henry's absence.

While I work, Able quietly discusses with me what supplies we need, and how much I should expect to pay for some of the items. Gabriela's approach sends him scurrying into a stall, but I keep forking hay to a friendly ass as she enters. Seeing me doing her husband's chores brings a smile to her face, and it makes me feel good when she showers me with gratitude. The smell of hot pottage and fresh baked bread makes my mouth water, and I can hear the rustle of straw as the others begin to wake up from the aroma of the food.

When everything has been brought out, she tells me to call for her when we are finished. My thoughtfulness earns me a huge piece of pie smothered in rich cream, and a hug that nearly crushes my ribs. When she leaves, Able comes out of hiding, and calls for the others to come and get it. We discuss our supply list while we eat, and savor every mouthful of her wonderful food until there isn't a crumb left for even a mouse.

When the list is complete, Able asks everyone how much they can contribute to the cost of the supplies. His eyes nearly pop out of his head when Ruby and Sapphire plunk down, and then dump a sack of coins that could have ransomed a princess.

"Where did you come by all that?" he asks breathlessly. He looks like he is going to faint.

"We inherited most of it from our mother, but Pappy, the old man who had taken us in after her death, had also set aside some coin for us."

I've never seen so much coin in one place in my whole life, and I know my eyes are as big as the others as we stare it. Sybal produces a modest pile, and so does Able, but of the piles, my pathetic stack of coins is the least. Able subtracts an equal amount of coins from everyone's pile, which leaves me nearly none, and strongly advises the twins against showing or telling anyone about their wealth.

"Do we have enough to buy a pack animal?" Ruby asks hopefully.

"Sapphire and I have already talked about buying one, and we'd be happy to buy one for the journey if you think we need it."

Able thinks about it, and discusses it with us. There are a lot of advantages to having a pack animal, and there are also a lot of disadvantages as well, but after some discussion, it is decided that we will try to find one if we can secure a reasonable price.

"Scamper quit!" Ruby scolds, jerking the scrawny squirrel out of her robe by the scruff of its neck.

She realizes her mistake too late, and looks at Able. I can see her relief when he merely shakes his head at her, and rolls his eyes skyward.

"I couldn't leave the poor thing, besides; I don't think he'll let me. It's like he's adopted me or something, and I figure it will be easier to hide him than deal with him popping up unexpectedly somewhere."

Able lets the matter drop and wipes off his eating knife, and trencher with a corner of his garment. I stack the empty ale pitcher, and pot on the platter, and am preparing to take them to Gabriela when shouts from the returning hunting party erupt in the street. The shouts carry the report of total victory over the hobgoblins, and it isn't long before people begin gathering in the street to celebrate the triumphant news. Able urges me to go learn what is happening, and shoos the others back into their stalls.

"We run 'em right into a cavalry unit, and they were wiped out to a beast," one man shouts.

"Didn't lose any men, but we did have a few minor injuries," Henry confesses after suffering through an emotional reunion with Gabriela.

I talk with Henry a little while out by his wood pile, and he shares several tankards of ale with me when he finds out he doesn't have any chores to do. The ale makes him more affable, and by the time I leave, I've secured his help the following day in helping me get the supplies we need. In return, I promise I will be his guest at the Solstice festival the next night. He won't accept no for an answer, and insists that I allow my family at least one more day to rest.

"How could I refuse," I tell Able when I return, "he's even putting us up for free."

I've been worried about how Able would take the news, but he assures me I've done the right thing.

"No, you did good Zeke. We're safe here, and he's right about the girls needing the rest. I would have done the same. Look, I'm going to turn in. Stand a two hour watch, and then wake up Ruby. I don't think we'll need more than one person to guard us during our stay. Have Ruby wake Sapphire, then me. Sybal didn't look too good at supper, so I don't want her disturbed. I know she'll protest the special treatment, but I figure she'll get over it."

We share a laugh, and Able goes to bed. I can't help thinking that he too needs some rest. Dark circles have appeared under his eyes, and

I notice he isn't nearly as cheerful as he'd been when we first met. I seem to be making a habit out of making decisions, and when I wake Ruby for her watch, she agrees we need to let them both catch up on their rest.

The next day Henry helps me find all the supplies we need, and I notice that with his presence, the prices are very good. Animals are as scarce as coins, but we did succeed in buying a rather old ox before the day was out. My coin pouch still holds a fair amount of coins when I show my purchases to the others, and to my surprise, everyone insists I keep them since I have the least amount of money. I am about to repeat my famous little jig, but Sybal grabs my leg, and stops me.

"Stick to the harp, you'll live longer," she advises.

I could tell she's feeling better because her sense of humor has returned. I don't think anyone hears me when I try to express my gratitude for their generosity because they are laughing so hard at her joke.

That night, my *wife* and I, spend a pleasant evening enjoying the festival. Hundreds have gathered around the large fire, and Gabriela informs me that many people have traveled long distances to be here. I decide to leave my harp behind tonight, because I entertain other ideas on how I want to spend my time with Ruby. Maybe I'll get lucky, or at least I am hoping to get lucky. I *need* to get lucky.

After the leaping contest, which I did not do so well at, a group of men began playing some lively music. My prowess with dancing has not impressed Ruby enough to allow me the privilege of escorting her to the dance area. But though she refuses to dance with me during the fast dances, I secure a promise from her that she'll dance the slower ones with me. The ale really begins to flow, and we drink our fill. We both are pleasantly plowed by the time the music slows, but Ruby keeps her promise, and we join the others.

She shyly comes into my arms as the music begins to play, but refuses to let me draw her in close to my body. Surprisingly, we move well together, and by the third dance, and as many tankards of ale, she is becoming more relaxed. She is pressed tight against me by this time, laughing, and teasing me mercilessly as we dance. Her close softness makes me giddy, and I can't stop my hands from wandering. Though she does remove them from her backside a few times, she has not become too upset with my tactics, and my courage strengthens.

I've noticed couples kissing at the end of the music, and think to myself to press my luck further. When the music ends, I continue to hold her, though she expects to be released. She looks up at me, and I can tell she knows what I am about to do, yet she doesn't try to pull away. My heart is thudding like a war drum, and I can feel her trembling when I lean in. Our eyes never waver when our lips meet, and it is as if we are the only two people in the world while it lasts. When reality returns, the shyness does too, and Ruby quickly drops her eyes. I want more, much more, but suddenly she isn't as receptive to my needs as I was hoping she'd be, and I am thwarted whenever I try to kiss her again.

We have to leave the festival long before it ends, but not before saying our heartfelt thanks and goodbyes to our kindly hosts. We are leaving before first light, and we know our hosts will just be getting to bed by that time, because festivals like these usually last all night long. I lose my last chance to attempt another kiss from Ruby, because Able greets us at the barn door with a grin that tells me he's been spying on us. I could have brained him. Ruby must have interpreted his grin too, because she hurries away without saying a word to either of us. Able tells me to go get some rest after dodging several of my attempts to knock his head off, and seeing that it is no use, I comply. I can't sleep. I am too frustrated with pent up emotions for sleep to come easy, and besides, I am also trying to overhear what Ruby is telling the other two women. I can't overhear a thing except occasional giggling, and snickering laughter. It's unnerving.

The next morning as we walk down the dark quiet street, nothing remains of the fire but glowing embers. Able had taken the time to update his map from what I had learned from Henry about the area, and after a final reviewing of it, he puts the map away. Henry had been a wealth of information because he had traveled with the king's army on several campaigns that led to the border of Wynelvenest. With the new updates, Able decides that we will try to gain back lost time by staying on a new, but less used road. We haven't traveled but a few hours when Able calls a halt, and mysteriously begins grinning at the women.

"The girls haven't been idle while you've been out handling our affairs," he ventures, suddenly bashful. Baffled, I watch them remove a very bulky blanket from the ox. Ruby literally staggers under the weight of it as she brings it over to me, and lays it at my feet.

"Here, I fixed something up for you, but it's Sybal's idea," she states as if she doesn't want me to read anything into it, but her anticipation leads me to believe she's put a lot of effort into whatever it is she's done. I unroll the blanket and find various pieces of the recovered hobgoblins armor wrapped up within it. It has been cleaned, shined, and patched. Sapphire and Sybal have smug expressions on their faces, and Able is trying too hard not to show any expression at all.

"Well, try it on," Ruby says anxiously.

Able helps me put on the breastplate, shoulder piece, arm brassards, thigh cuisses, and lower leg greaves. The helm they've chosen, from the three helms we had taken from the dead hobgoblins, fits perfectly. When I am finished putting the armor on, I tie my sword belt into place, heft the heavy shield, and Able steps back so the others can see.

The armor is a little loose in places, but not enough to be bothersome. I am still growing, so it won't be any time at all before the armor fits properly.

"You'll get use to the weight, and before long, you'll not even notice it," Able laughs as I struggle to walk.

Ruby dodges my thanks like she's dodged my attempts to try and kiss her again, but I can tell she is immensely pleased with herself. Within an hour of resuming our journey, I am sweating profusely, chafed, and thoroughly miserable, but Able refuses to let me remove any of the cumbersome items. We don't encounter a soul on the road this day, and to heighten my discomfort, it is stifling hot. By evening I am wishing I am dead, and am about ready to chunk this gear into the nearest river. I wouldn't give a damn if I hurt Ruby's feelings at this point. We camp well off the road this night, and by the time our weapons practice is over, I can barely move at all.

Able kindly gives me a salve to ease my discomfort, and I try especially hard to convince Ruby to rub the ointment on me, but my suggestion is warded off so venomously, that I am left wondering if I've misinterpreted her feelings for me. Her disposition makes me mad clean through, and I decide that if she is going to have an attitude like that, I'll ask Sybal. Sybal is more than happy to oblige, but as we disappear into my tent, Able shoots me a look that clearly states he isn't at all pleased with this new development.

CHAPTER TWENTY

Between a Rock and a Deep Place

The flap to my tent has barely settled into place behind us when it is jerked open again by a wild eyed, demon possessed, and very angry Ruby. Sybal has knelt to help me take off my greaves, but is suddenly jerked out of the tent by both ears before she can even lay a finger on the first buckle. Thinking it very wise not to step out of the tent, I peek out the flap.

I've seen a cat fight or two between my sisters on the farm, but the way these two were going at it, beat the hell out the tussles I'd witnessed in the past. Come to think of it, I hadn't seen too many fights amongst men that had been this brutal. It is taking everything Able has to hold Sapphire back, and from the look on her face, I'm not too sure who she is pulling for. Ruby gets the upper hand by pulling Sybal plumb off her feet. The move is so skillfully performed that Sybal doesn't see it coming. Ruby swiftly ducks beneath Sybal's flailing arms, grabs her by the ankles, and yanks. Sybal lands hard on her back, the wind knocked from her. In a flash, Ruby straddles Sybal across her chest and arms, using her weight advantage to keep the woman pinned down.

Ruby starts raining down closed fisted blows on Sybal's unprotected face, and several land so hard, they knock the spunk right out of the smaller woman. Seeing its master getting the upper hand in the battle, the squirrel also begins attacking the downed elf. I step out of the tent to break it up the moment I hear Sybal calling out in submission. I've done this a time or two in the past, and know that one has to be very cautious when interfering with someone who is as upset as Ruby is.

As expected, when I bear-hug her from behind, Ruby begins

kicking and screaming in a very unladylike fashion, but I do succeed in lifting her off of Sybal. I let her go when she settles down, and before the angry squirrel begins attacking me next. To my surprise, she goes immediately over to Sybal to apologize, and helps the elf up. Able lets Sapphire go too, and before she rushes over to join the other women, she angrily kicks Able in the leg. Able limps over to me rubbing his shin, and he seems as confused as I am when they all began hugging each other.

Able tries to warn me too late as I start to walk over to join the girls, but I realize my mistake immediately when they all turn to glare at me before I can even approach. I stop when I am met with a united front of angry stares and scornful looks. The damn squirrel even bares his teeth at me. Then Ruby, crosses the short span between us, and slaps my face so hard, my ears are still ringing well after the three of them march past me and go into one of the tents together. Luckily, the squirrel only gets a mouth full of steel when he tries to bite my ankle. It flees from me before I can stomp him right good, and all I get for the effort is a flash of bushy tale as it joins the others in the tent.

I turn towards Able for consolation, but Able is nowhere to be found, and I swear I hear muffled laughter coming from somewhere in the darkness. Sapphire, and Sybal emerge from the tent to resume the watch, but neither of them even glance my direction. Disconcerted, and desperately needing to rub some salve on the places where the armor has chafed me, I return to my tent, light a candle, and begin to undress. Undressing is not an easy task, and as much pain as I am in, I desperately need Able's help. I am cursing up a storm when the curtain suddenly opens, and Ruby steps in.

"Well, close your mouth before you attract the flies in here," she commands. "I would have scratched at the door, but since your flap is gapped open wide enough for the whole world to see in, I didn't think it was necessary. Turn around, and let me help you get that off. Turn around, and don't be getting any of your ideas either."

What else am I suppose to do? I turn around. Neither of us speaks as she deftly removes my armor pieces, and since I am confused by her sudden change in mood, I think it is prudent to not push my untrustworthy luck.

"You presume too much, sir," Ruby warns me when I begin to shuck my trousers.

Mortified by her chastisement, I freeze. She's helped me out of my shirt, so how the hell was I supposed to know she wasn't going to help me out of the rest of my clothes? Embarrassed, and expecting her to storm out of the tent, I actually flinch when the cool salve on her fingers touches a raw place on my back. The salve instantly eases the pain, and the more she applies to the chafed places, the better I begin to feel. Thinking that all is forgiven, I begin entertaining thoughts about enticing her into kissing me again. When she has me turn around, thoughts of this nature vanish completely. I am unnerved because she is staring right at my crotch, and then she breaks into a fit of uncontrollable laughter. To make matters worse, Able sticks his head in to see what is going on. Seeing Ruby, he withdraws it, but not before he too bursts into a fit of laughter. Glancing down, I cringe. I cover myself with both hands, but the damage is done. In the blink of an eye, a red-faced Ruby hastens out of the tent.

During my watch, my feelings are on where I can find a cavern dark enough to mask my monstrous shame regarding the embarrassing incident. These thoughts and more plague me as it draws close to the hour when everyone would start to get up. Able rags me the entire time he stands watch with me, and had he not been so quick on his feet, I think I really would have run him through with my sword. I am dreading the next few hours, and would rather be beaten with a blacksmiths anvil than have to face the three women when they emerge from their tents. When the moment of truth arrives, it isn't as bad as I am thinking, or maybe it is worse. Either way, it is unsettling, and though I act like I am perfectly happy with the way they act towards me that morning, I am also still left thinking troubled thoughts as to the absence of their mockery.

We travel for a day and a half without encountering anyone upon the road. Deciding we need to increase our progress by staying on the road, Able makes a few more changes in how we travel. Though it is dangerous, he and Sybal begin walking far ahead of us. This enables them to scout the lay of the land, and if need be, warn us when to get off the road when they see someone traveling towards us. If we encounter a village, or a town, I am sent in to learn all I can of the area, obtain the latest news, and purchase supplies if we need them.

During my absence, the party would skirt the area, and meet up with me on the road just beyond the populated area. If the road happens to go through fields where people are working, we would circle far enough around them to avoid being seen. This way of traveling slows us, but not as much as we would be slowed traveling in the wilder regions. Several times we come to crossroads that branch off to the east and west, but we continue to go steadily north. Just when we begin to wonder how much farther it will be before we will reach Hadrian's Wall, and the border of Wynelvenest, we meet up with a trader who is able to give us good information.

While the others hide, I am able to learn that we are only a couple days from the border. When I tell the trader that I am determined to see Hadrian's Wall, he looks at me as if I am crazy, and does his best to dissuade me.

"These are dangerous times," he warns, "There's unrest in the kingdoms, talk of war with the elves, robbery by highwaymen, and raids by barbarians. Tis not a good time to be wandering the roads, minstrel, so don't be put out if folks be treating you unkindly. They be scared and desperate these days. The overlord's taxes be crushing their backs, men and boys be taken from their farms to fight for the nobles, and I've heard some say strange creatures have been attacking areas that have been left unprotected as the king moves troops north."

His information is far from heartening, and when we part ways, I am beginning to have serious doubts about this adventure. We leave the road, and begin walking through meadows of intense beauty. By noon, the sun has been blotted out by clouds, and a stiff breeze begins to blow. We take a cold meal at the edge of a dense forest where mists swirl, and shadows loom. It's quite a spooky scene. Able keeps eyeing the forest nervously and I can tell he doesn't want to go within its creepy interior. Resigned to the fact that there are no other alternatives but to enter the forest, he leads us into the mists.

"Keep together," he orders.

Our visibility is becoming obscured to the point we can barely see the person in front of us.

"Able," Sybal calls, interrupting Ruby's lesson, and bringing us to another halt, "You are beginning to stray off course. I think you'd better let me lead us for a while. If this wind gets any stronger, we might need to find shelter. I also think we should tie a short rope from one person to the next so we do not become separated."

Able agrees, and Sybal takes the lead. The wind is becoming fierce, and some of the stronger gusts make me grab Able by his shirt to keep him from being blown off his feet. I lose all track of time as we walk, and I guess it is nearly an hour before Sybal stops again. We group around her so she doesn't have to shout over the howling wind, and listen carefully.

"Able, there is a building up ahead. Do you want to check it out?"

Able nods his head and Sybal leads us through the swirling mists to where she's spotted the structure. The moaning wind is giving me the creeps, and even the ox seems skittish. When the building comes into view, its eerie opening doesn't look very welcoming, and even Able seems tentative about approaching it. The structure isn't a building, but an enclosed vaulted archway of granite with wide stone steps leading down into what might be a long forgotten crypt.

"Zeke, come with me. You three stay here, we'll be right back,"

Able shouts over the wind.

Able takes the time to cut two stout staffs from a nearby tree, and struggles to light a torch he'd taken from a pack on the ox. He finally gets it to light, and then hands me the torch, and one of the staffs.

"Whatever you do, drop the staff and not the torch if you need to draw your weapon. Use the staff to test the ground in front of you as you walk. If there are any traps, there is a slight chance you might avoid getting hurt."

I want to tell him that if I don't go into the creepy place to begin with, I wouldn't need to worry about traps, but I know it won't do me any good. He is overflowing with excitement, and I am just hoping my boots don't overflow with piss.

Able draws his sword, and taps the first step with his staff. We test every step this way as we descend into the gloomy depths, but nothing out of the ordinary occurs. Many times I am forced to burn thick strands of ancient cobwebs, and twice bats swarm us when the light disturbs their rest. We can't see the rats, but we can hear them scurrying back and forth in the shadows below us. The steps seem to go on forever, and gradually we leave behind the sounds from above. Every noise we make sounds too loud and every sound we hear causes us to jump.

The wide stairs end in what appears to be an atrium. We explore the atrium, and find it to be nearly four rods in length, and a rod in width and height. On the other side of the atrium, and barring our entry to what lies beyond it, is a burnished bronze door. A cross is emblazoned on the door, and on each side of the cross are inscriptions. The inscriptions are symbols or letters written in a language I have seen before, but am unable to read. To the left of the cross is inscribed the letters ἄλφα, and on the right, ὦ μέγα.

"I believe this is written in the language of the Romans or the Greeks, but I am not sure," Able claims after closely examining the symbols.

We try to open the doors, but they won't budge, nor can Able discover a device that will trigger them into opening.

"Well," he says in frustration, "It's of no use, and we need to return to the others before they become worried. I think it will be safe to weather out the storm down here, and get some rest. The steps are wide, so I think we can even coax the ox into coming down them."

Nodding, though I don't savor the idea of spending any more time down here at all, I follow him back across the atrium, and back up the stairs. Not far from the entrance, we encounter a very worried Sybal coming down the steps.

"I was worried something may have happened to you," she claims when we ascend to where she waits.

"Tis a good ways down, but there is a nice area below where we can ride out the storm," Able relays.

The twins are overjoyed to see us, and once Able explains his intentions, we begin the descent. The ox is more than willing to get out of the storm, and we have no problem getting him to go down the stairs. When we enter the atrium, Able is happier than a hog at sloppin' time, and eagerly begins showing everyone what we have discovered. Seeing the writing on the doors, Sybal walks over and begins studying them.

"Able, the writing says the beginning, and the end. It is written in…"

Before Sybal can finish, she is cut off by a deep rumbling sound that comes from behind us. I am immensely impressed with how quickly I draw my sword, and notice the others are quickly reacting as well. The rumbling is followed by a grating sound that makes my skin crawl.

"What's going on?" Ruby asks in a voice that quakes as bad as my knees.

"Come!" Able yells over the noise. Slowly he advances towards the stairs. "Hold your torches high so I can see!" he cries.

I lift my torch, and Sybal does the same, but the torches will only cast their flickering light just shy of a rod. The atrium's length is now a disadvantage as we creep forward, and the once friendly light from our torches now casts shadows that dance around us like lively wraiths.

"I don't like this!" Able shouts out, and increases his pace.

When the area of where the staircase should be comes into view, we know we are doomed, and though we break into a run, it is far too late to react. We have been sealed within…

CPSIA information can be obtained at www.ICGtesting.com
Printed in the USA
LVOW082350301211

261769LV00002B/239/P